the V

Vanishin

Po

the Vanishing Point

A STORY OF LAVINIA FONTANA

A NOVEL BY

Louise Hawes

 Houghton Mifflin Company Boston 2004

www.houghtonmifflinbooks.com

The text of this book is set in Centaur.

Library of Congress Cataloging-in-Publication Data

Hawes, Louise.
The vanishing point : a story of Lavinia Fontana / by Louise Hawes.
p. cm.
Summary: Presents the story of a young girl of Bologna who worked in her father's
all-male painting studio and came to enjoy more fame than any female artist before her.

ISBN-13: 978-0-618-43423-7
ISBN-10: 0-618-43423-2

1. Fontana, Lavinia, 1552-1614—Juvenile fiction. [1. Fontana, Lavinia, 1552-1614—Fiction.
2. Painters—Fiction. 3. Sex role—Fiction.
4. Bologna (Italy)—History—Papal rule, 1506-1797—Fiction.] I. Title.
PZ7.H3126Van 2004
[Fic]—dc22
2004007573

Manufactured in the United States of America
MP 10 9 8 7 6 5 4 3 2 1

For Isabel and Maurice,
who helped me balance head and heart

...from the center of my life came
a great fountain, deep, blue
shadows on azure seawater.

—Louise Glück,
The Wild Iris

Thanks

are due many "dear hearts and gentle people." I hope this acknowledgment pays a small part of the debt I owe my sisters in WINC (Writers and Illustrators of North Carolina), especially Luli, who helped find this book a home, and Frances, my wondrous First Reader; the National Museum of Women in the Arts, for mounting the exhibition that inspired my novel; Dr. Stephen Foster, professor of ophthalmology at Harvard Medical School; Stanton Thomas, assistant curator of paintings at the Cleveland Museum of Art; the good padre at Santissima Trinità in Bologna; Helen, who taught me about blind drawing; Kate O'Sullivan, my intrepid editor; and my students and colleagues in the Vermont College MFA in Writing for Children and Young Adults Program. Bless you, every one.

Historical Characters

LAVINIA FONTANA, called Vini, daughter of Antonia and Prospero.

ANTONIA DE' BONARDIS, daughter of a printer, wife of Prospero Fontana, mother of Lavinia.

PROSPERO FONTANA, husband of Antonia, father of Lavinia, respected portraitist with a thriving studio in Bologna.

GIAN PAOLO ZAPPI, a student in Prospero's studio.

LUDOVICO CARRACCI, another student of Prospero Fontana, later to found a famous art studio with his brother and cousin.

ULISSE ALDROVANDI, a well-known natural scientist, author of an encyclopedia.

CARLO SIGONIO, a professor at the University of Bologna

Historical Characters

CATERINA VIGRI of Bologna, legendary fifteenth-century artist and founder of a Poor Clares monastery, later the city's patron saint.

SOFONISBA ANGUISSOLA, daughter of a wealthy family from Cremona, who gained fame as a painter while Lavinia was growing up.

MICHELANGELO BUONARROTI, famous Renaissance artist who died when Lavinia was twelve years old, said to have corresponded with Anguissola.

CATERINA DE' MEDICI, Florentine noblewoman who became queen of France and ruled as regent during Lavinia's adolescence.

NOVELLA CALDERINI, fourteenth-century noblewoman who lectured in law at the University of Bologna.

Fictional Characters

Anatole Riggio, Beatrice, Ginevra, Pietro Catanio, and Father Anselmo are not patterned on historical figures. Similarly, Silvana, the Gypsy cook; her daughter, Betta; Giorgio, the groom; and the other servants in the Fontana household, are not actual people. But these characters, or men and women very like them, surely lived and toiled, unrecorded, among the sixty thousand inhabitants of sixteenth-century Bologna.

Her dream arms moved as if she had worked puppets all her life. Like God in Heaven, she looked down from above. The puppets' strings were swallowed in a shaft of sunlight, so the princess and the dragon appeared to be walking and talking on their own.

She spoke the princess's words, but the dragon's growl came from the man beside her; she could feel the pressure of his shoulder against hers and hear his gruff whisper as he flapped the dragon's wings. "Buono," he told her as the marionettes danced. "Molto buono. You are blessed with a great gift."

Then the dream broke like a bubble, and she was no longer working the puppets; now she was one of them. She heard her silk skirts rustle and delighted in the green slippers that peeked daintily from underneath her hem. She laughed at the dragon's roar and invited him to stop breathing fire and dance with her instead. They leaped and chased each other around the stage like playful squirrels, then bowed low as the sound of applause washed over them.

But as the clapping and stamping died down, she felt herself torn from the light and suddenly upended. She was left in the stillness behind musty stage curtains, her strings taut, her legs stretched awkwardly above her head. "Always hang them upside down," she heard a deep voice caution. "Otherwise, they may come to life when you are not looking."

Chapter One

IT IS RAINING. AGAIN. VINI'S SHEETS FEEL STICKY, MOLDED INTO ridges that send shivers of irritation through her legs and arms. The curtains around her bed hang limp and spiritless. She will not get up.

"*Vieni*, Vini!"

She will not open those curtains on another dull morning, on her mother's pale face.

"Come on, Lavinia!"

She turns over, muffling Antonia's voice and the hollow splatter of drops in the cistern outside the window. But it is too late. Her dream, like someone she knows but whose name she has forgotten, cannot be called back.

She peeks through the curtains at the floor. Her mother and her aunt wove the rug by her bed during the "waiting months" before she was born. On one side, the head of a huge, snarling griffin, its eyes the color of fire, looks back toward its tail. Or perhaps toward the small dove nestled comfortably under its scaled wings. At the bottom, a small scroll clutched in the griffin's talons announces the year of Vini's birth, 1552.

She supposes that the dove was once white, but ever since she was little, she has gotten out of bed in the middle of the rug. The small bird is now slate colored, nearly worn away from hundreds of her groggy, morning footprints. Over and over, Vini has considered changing her waking ritual to spare the vanishing bird. But even at fourteen, she cannot bring herself to step on the griffin's blood-colored jaws or tangled fur.

"Vini, my love." Antonia's tone is awkward, suppliant. She has come into the room now, and Vini can see her slippers under the curtain, the hesitant way they are set, just inside the door. "Do you want to read Latin on an empty stomach?"

Dry lessons. Wet rain. And a dream that is now as faded and colorless as the poor little dove on her rug. Vini sits up, listening for her mother's sigh, her retreating footsteps. Cautiously, she draws the bed curtains apart and finds that someone is still in the room.

"Cesare!" She laughs as the tiny dog, named after Julius Caesar, digs its claws into her sheets and scrabbles onto her bed. "Cesare, you will have to eat less to spare my linens." The dog rolls onto its back, wriggling in ecstasy as she scratches its fat belly. "These sheets will be in shreds unless you lose weight or learn to fly!"

Then, with Cesare dancing around her ankles, Vini gets out of bed and takes the chamber pot from her close-chair. She has no inclination to expose herself to this cold and unpromising morning. She slips the pot under her nightshirt, holding it close. If things go on this way, she thinks, there will be no puppets in the square again today. It was just after Saint John's Day she saw them last. Unless the sun finds its way back to Bologna, she will never finish her picture.

She pulls a green woolen dress over her shirt and scowls into the mirror while she combs her hair. Soon, though, she remembers the puppet show and uses her comb for a sword, slashing the air in a frenzy. "Ha! Infidels!" she says, checking the curl of her lip in the glass. "I will defend Christendom to the death!"

Cesare is delighted with her performance, yelping his approval and whirling on his back feet in tight, crazy circles. But Vini, instead of encouraging his dance, whispers morning prayers and hurries downstairs to the kitchen.

Between bites of porridge, and later during her lessons with Anatole Riggio, she checks the sky. Before each conjugation, she notes with despair that the heavy drops are still falling. As they begin Virgil, she listens hopelessly to the sound behind her tutor's reedy voice, the weary, constant hammer of rain.

For weeks now, Vini and her teacher have been translating the scene where Lavinia, Aeneas's second wife, learns of the blood that has been shed in her name. Perhaps Signor Riggio thinks Vini will yawn less if her lessons involve a namesake. Or maybe the old scholar, his hands trembling as he turns the pages, the lead weights of his glasses shivering behind his ears, fancies flying limbs and gouged sides.

But for Vini, reading about battles and romance is not the same as *seeing* them. Not the same as sneaking out of the house, a scarf tied around her head like a maid on errands. Not at all the same as standing with the crowd around the puppet stage where princesses and warriors, kings and flying serpents come to life.

And so it seems the answer to a prayer she has not dared speak, when the sun comes out after the midday meal. To ask God to stop the rain, when you are not a saint and can too easily confuse your will with His, would be wrong. But to slip out during *riposa*, when the whole house is napping, to hurry down the street, glorying in the new light, feels as right as anything Vini has ever done.

By the time she ties Cesare up so he cannot follow her and walks to the square off Piazza San Francesco, the play is already under way. She works slowly through the hundreds of bodies packed around the stage until she can see. Clearly this show is not a continuation of the romantic legend the puppeteers performed last time they were in town.

Today two elegantly dressed puppets, bent on destroying each other, race up and down in front of a backdrop painted to look like the reception hall of a great palace. One of the puppets is at a distinct disadvantage, and when they stop their mad scramble for a moment, Vini sees that it is the man.

The hapless duke tries once again to escape his lady's temper. But his wife, despite her long brocade gown and jeweled robe, is too quick for him. She is on him in an instant, pummeling him with her fists.

All around her, Vini hears the laughter. Like a wave gathering force, it lifts her, tugs at her until she too begins to smile, then to laugh out loud with the rest of the audience. Onstage, though, no one is laughing. A courtier rushes out from behind the velvet curtains to help the beleaguered duke. "*Signore mio,*" he calls, "I am coming. I will save you."

But the duke has decided, apparently, to save himself. He drops to his knees and, in a highly ignoble whine, makes one promise after another. "I will give you my finest horse," he tells the duchess. "I will send you to Rome to visit your mother. I will have your portrait painted in gold leaf and your image struck on a medal to wear around my neck."

His wife stops her attack for an instant, and that is all the time the crafty duke requires. Suddenly he is on his feet again, tearing across the stage, his tormentor in hot pursuit. Back and forth the two of them run, the woman carrying a stick now and a fresh scene unscrolling across the painted backdrop behind them. Instead of the duke's grand palace, this new painting features a landscape, tumbling green hills with small houses and grazing sheep clustered on their slopes.

"You'd better run fast, fellow," a man yells from the crowd. His voice has an edge, a harshness that almost makes Vini turn to look at him. But she cannot leave the colors on the stage: the sky on the silk backdrop is as blue as a thrush egg; the duchess's necklace and the gold trim on her gown flash as she runs; the glass emeralds on the curtains catch the sun and throw patches of light, like fluttering butterflies, across the stage.

"If your wife is anything like mine," the same man cries out again, "she'll run you into the ground, you poor dumb fox."

There is more laughter, and others begin to yell, too. "Courage, brother!" a second man says. "Don't let us down," cries a third.

The curtain closes and the laughter turns to applause. Stamping and clapping erupt behind her, but Vini is still watching the stage. The puppeteers come out in front now, and each holds the strings of the marionettes he worked during the performance.

As usual, Vini is too stunned to clap. She stands, watching the four men who loom like giants beside the tiny stage that, only seconds ago, was big enough to hold the world. It is always the same, this shock, this coming down—as if a bird has fallen from the sky and landed at her feet. The duchess, that savage, sparkling woman with cloud-colored hair, is actually no longer than Vini's arm. Her noble husband the duke lies crumpled and spineless against the ankles of the man who holds his strings.

"Thank you, ladies and gentlemen of Bologna." One of the puppeteers, older and stouter than the rest, shouts after the crowd, which is already drifting into the streets that fan like wheel spokes from the cobblestone square. "Even in Ravenna," the man tells them, his hands cupped around his mouth, his voice louder than any of the puppets', "there are no more generous souls. If by chance you have neglected to feed my hungry hat, and if you enjoyed our little play, let your lire speak for you now."

A few people near the stage drop money into the wide-brimmed hat that lies, half full, at the man's feet. One woman smiles and curtsies like a shy child as she tosses in her coin. But Vini has neither smiles nor coins to contribute. She turns from the stage, brimming with a sweet, not unpleasant sadness, which she nurses all the way home.

Look at me, she scolds herself. *I am nearly fifteen, too old to cry.* But the magic is over and now she must go home. Home to the dreary, full-size world. To her mother, who would never argue with her father, much less take after him with a stick. To her father, who has never, so far as Vini knows, given her mother a gift. *What would Mama do with one of Papa's horses, anyway? They are all trained to respond to his hand and his alone. And why on earth would Prospero Fontana paint a portrait of his own wife, when he is paid so handsomely to paint the wives of others?*

Chapter Two

VINI SLOWS AS SOON AS SHE REACHES VIA SANTO STEFANO. SHE takes her time approaching the house, like someone slipping into a cold bath. Carefully, she closes the front gate. The ground, even the walls, are slick from this morning's rain, but the prodigal sun has turned the fountain at the center of the courtyard into a reflecting pool.

Vini does not spend long watching herself there, just enough time to smooth her hair, to tuck her scarf into the sleeve of her gown. Then she passes the kitchen and, as always, peeks in the window of her father's workshop.

Today she does not see Prospero Fontana, only his students, perched around the long table they use for meals and for work. In the center is a dusty clay vase with two handles just above its swollen hips.

Even if he is not visible, her father is evident in the worshipful, anxious gaze all the young men direct toward a corner of the room

Vini cannot see through the window. Some of the students nod, then lower their heads and begin to scratch their charcoal sticks across the thick papers in front of them.

No, she has not heard him. But Vini knows exactly what her father has just said, what he is forever saying. "Paint first with your eyes. Use them like hands, *garzoni.*" He calls them boys, though nearly all are men. "Caress every curve, every corner."

And she knows, too, that the students who have already started drawing will soon be sorry. "You did not look first, did you?" her father will ask. "You think you know *this* vase just because you have seen others?"

And he will stand behind them, each in turn, leaving one hand on their shoulder while he points to their sketch with the other. "I found this amphora in Calabria. See where it has been oiled to hold the water? Did you show that in your drawing? And here, where one handle has thinned from being carried day after day, year after year? Have you shown this, too?"

Of course, those eager hares will shake their heads, will look shamefaced, while the triumphant tortoises will smile as if they've known the secret all along. A play Vini knows by heart, it is all happening the same way again today. Her father has moved into sight now, is walking purposefully toward Paolo Zappi, the new shop boy who is allowed to sketch with the apprentices. Prospero sweeps past the window; his great shoulders and broad back fill its frame, his dark mane trembles as he shakes his head.

Vini ducks under the window, listens to the familiar, reproachful growl. "*Adesso, artiste,* let us try again." She knows how tenderly her father has draped his arm around Paolo, who is neither hare nor tortoise but more like a bumbling pony, with arms and legs he has not yet mastered. "Draw this beautiful form with your eyes, do not touch your paper."

Paolo is a good-natured fellow, the sort Vini knows she can rely on; the sort Prospero makes a habit of singling out. "Do you see here, good Sir, where you have imposed your dream of a jar on what's before you?" Paolo nods, and Vini feels in her own body the sting, the small poisoned barb of her father's disapproval.

"We will not give up hope, however," Prospero is saying. "Even the unlikeliest among us can learn to see. Begin at the bottom, there, then worship every inch, every change of hue . . ."

Vini shakes out her gown and scuttles back to the kitchen door, opens it as if she has just come in from the courtyard. Silvana is stirring something in the big soup pot, and Vini cannot resist tickling the old woman around her broad waist. The smells of saffron and stock-drenched rice rise off Silvana like a heady dew as she giggles, then turns from the hearth to threaten Vini with her spoon.

"For pity's sake, do not bother Silvana." Vini's mother, Cesare nestled like a miniature sultan in her arms, hurries across the room and plants herself between Vini and the maid, as if she is separating lovers. "You know how she overseasons. Even without your help."

Antonia Fontana, her daughter is sure, actually loves the thick, garlic-laced dishes their ancient maid always produces unless someone watches her closely. It is not for herself or for Vini, then, that Antonia is standing guard. It is to prevent another scene like the one last night.

"Subtlety, my soul mate," Prospero told Vini's mother as soon as he tasted the fish at dinner, "is not one of your virtues, it seems."

"My dear?" Antonia had leaned across the table, her meal untouched, her eyes trained on his with the same expectant, anxious look his students always wear. Signora Fontana is a thin woman, with skin as white as the ruffs she wears at her throat, but whenever she looks at her husband, even after all these years, she blushes.

"There is an art to supervising the preparation of a meal," Vini's father announced, "just as there is to enjoying it." He had looked at Vini then, had explained to her rather than to his wife. "It is my experience that people who pick at food the way your good mother does, have not the faintest idea how to make sure the taste of a dish is properly complemented. For them, it is always the same—garlic, garlic, garlic. Everything else is beyond them."

Antonia had started to reply, then settled instead for busying her hands under the table, twisting them around each other as if she were trying to keep warm.

"It requires imagination and a certain hardiness of spirit," Signor Fontana continued, sucking a fish bone already white as a fossil, "to appreciate the range of flavors sealed in each food." He dropped the bone, not on his dish but on the cloth beneath, where it formed a small, damp print of itself, a shadow bone.

"Unfortunately, the lady of this house suffers from thin blood. She lacks energy and nerve. She lacks the juice of life." He finally turned from Vini to stare at her mother.

Antonia braved his stern look for an instant, then dropped her head to watch her own hands scrambling, faster and faster, in her lap.

"Which is why, no doubt," Prospero continued, "your three brothers dried up in her womb and I am without a son." *Son.* The word is like a bell tolling across their lives. *Son. Son.* Vini hears its deep, sad peal behind all her father's complaints. Behind the burnt roast. Behind the overpaid servants, the thin sauce, the chipped mirrors.

Vini had wanted to reach over then and grab her mother's frantic hands, had wanted to hide them away. Other women—the ladies father paints—have plump, calm hands. They rest quietly, like contented pigeons, in the ladies' laps or on their Bibles.

Those ladies have big families. Daughters and sons. Sons who make their husbands happy, their sisters proud. How Vini hates those fleshless, frightened hands of Mama's. Every time she looks at them, she burns with shame.

Today, though, with just the three of them in this steamy kitchen, Antonia's hands are not nervous and she is spending all the words she has squirreled away. She sets Cesare free, then reaches out to cup her daughter's face as she chatters on. "Where have you been, minx? I was beginning to worry. Right, Silvana? And with good reason, too." She races ahead before the old servant can answer. "Look at that face, will you." She steps away, still holding Vini, smiling into her eyes. "So round and soft—just like a Madonna, is she not? Like a saint, no?"

Silvana nods, which is all the encouragement Antonia needs. "We should hire a guard to escort this treasure wherever she goes."

"Mama, I was just in the garden. I fell asleep in the sun."

Her head still full of the magic she watched in the square, Vini has no patience with her mother, with the desperate, needy words. Antonia wants so little—a hug, a laugh, a kiss beside her eyes. But Vini cannot give them to her. Not now. Not when she has to hold everything she has seen in her mind, every line, every shape. "If you do not need me until dinner," she says, unwrapping herself from her mother's embrace, kissing (she can do that much) the tips of Antonia's fingers, "I could practice my music for a while."

Bless the spinet. It is like a spell. Just mention it, and both her father and mother become easy and serene, as if the dainty instrument in the back room is the key to all their futures. As if Vini's being able to play it will make her attractive enough, elegant enough to marry into luxury and out of their anxious care.

Perhaps she should feel guilty, then, when she has crossed the courtyard, Cesare at her heels. When she has abandoned the forlorn dog outside the carved door of the music room. ("No, no," she says, her voice stern to let him know his claws and bouncing are not welcome.) When she is finally seated, not in the velvet chair by the spinet but at the drawing desk she has rigged up nearby.

Only a pair of rough boards placed over a chest, the desk is just wide enough for the vellum pages she "borrows" from Prospero's studio. In minutes, she has finished the sketch. Weeks ago, she laid in the crowded square and the puppet stage, its heavy curtains drawn aside. Now she fills it with the duke and his wife, the duchess's stick raised above her husband's head.

It is not a proper subject for art, she knows. Papa's clients would never pay for such a thing. But if you squint and stand far enough back from the page, you can imagine that the figures are like the ones in paintings at church, that theirs is a sacred quarrel, full of biblical import. And if you look behind them, past the city and the houses, you can see God's own handiwork, the hills, the sheep, and the sky. The sky Vini aches to paint the color of a thrush's egg.

Chapter Three

FATHER HAS DISMISSED HIS APPRENTICES FOR THEIR EVENING meal and, her heart thudding in the silence, Vini has the whole shop to herself. She sneaks into the center of the room and lets the smell of the oil paints fill her chest and her nose. It works like wine, only faster.

She does not know how to mix paints yet, and she has no place to store them if she could. Silvana or her mother would be sure to notice the smell, sure to tell her father.

Prospero Fontana expects his daughter to *love* art, not to *make* it. Vini's aunt has taught her to embroider and to dance; she has tutors for reading, for science, and for music. Already Prospero boasts that his daughter would make a better wife than half the full-grown women in Bologna.

But none of those women, Vini reminds herself, knows what this is like. A secret more beguiling than the puppet shows but sweat-stained, too. Solid and exotic at once, earthy and forbidden, this place where men roll up their sleeves, tie on aprons, and turn work into beauty.

Everywhere she looks, there is something she is not supposed to want, something she yearns for with a physical ache like hunger: the scaffolds that soar to the ceiling, that sway and tremble, like wings, when Paolo and the others climb to the top. Colored powders ground from earth and stone. (Father tells no one where he gets the clay for his ochre.) Turpentine, linseed oil, chalks, grease pencils. Plaster casts of arms and legs, torsos, and hands. Easels and rolls of canvas. Huge compasses, their metal legs gleaming from hooks on the wall; mirrors for reflecting drawings, the model's stand, urns, draperies. And, of course, sheet after sheet of paper, stacked in careless piles, pale faces hidden, waiting, dreaming.

She cannot help it. Vini slips three sticks of charcoal and a drawing pencil from a bin. Then a piece of white chalk, thick and full of promise. She rolls them all up in a handkerchief, tucks it under her skirt, then tiptoes back to the music room. She hides the tiny bundle with her drawing in the bottom drawer of the chest. And that is when she hears the footsteps.

She closes the drawer, then runs to the spinet. She flings herself on the instrument and plays faster and faster, not caring if the music is good or bad, so long as it fills up the space between her and the door.

Underneath the tumbling notes, her heart plays its own frantic

song. When the door opens and it is only Silvana, smelling delicious, a gravy stain shaped like a sow's ear on her apron front, Vini
stops playing. She smiles gratefully, stands up, and follows the
maid, leaving unfinished a tune that has no name, something she
will never play again.

All through the evening meal, through her father's endless fault-
finding and lectures, Vini thinks of her sketch. She will need still
more paper from the shop. The duchess puppet's great balloon of
a dress is not working; she will have to redraw it. Meanwhile, Papa
talks on and on about a visitor he is expecting in less than a week,
a *venerable* (this is one of his favorite words) archaeologist. Dottore
Pietro Catanio, Prospero informs Vini and her mother, is bringing
part of his sculpture collection all the way from Florence. Those
dull boys in the shop will finally have something to keep them
awake.

Vini remembers the way the duchess's skirts flew out behind
her, but it is so hard to make things move on a page, to pick a single, frozen moment that stands for everything. She only half hears
a story her father is telling now, some accident in the shop. It is
probably Paolo Zappi he describes, falling on the floor in a jum-
ble of paints and casts, a plaster face landing next to his own. "If
I could have traded that head for the other," Prospero says, "I
might get some work out of that bungler yet."

It is when he says this that Vini hears a sound she cannot

remember hearing in her father's presence. Antonia forgets herself and laughs. It is doomed, this tiny, rippling laugh, like a candle lit in the wind. But when it starts, Prospero gives Vini's mother a new look. It is almost as if he has never seen her before. He studies every line, every pore, and when he does, of course, the laughter stops.

Father shakes himself, as if coming out of a dream, then remembers what he has been discussing. "The boy's parents waited too long to choose a career for him. He is practically untrainable." He shrugs off the Zappi family, too, and leans forward, his fingers folded into a temple roof above the tablecloth. "But I have much more important news."

It is about the expedition he and Catanio are planning, a dig just outside Rome. "Of course, the jackals have already been there," he says, that special note of disdain in his voice, like a firm hand pushing back an unruly crowd. "But they do not know what to look for. You can be sure we will find a few precious shards, perhaps even some intact pottery if we go deep enough."

Vini tries to imagine her father's soft hands digging in dirt. He loves to wear heavy, gem-studded rings and keeps a large pitcher of water in the studio so he can scrub his nails on the way in and out. She can easily picture—sees every day, in fact—those long fingers pointing, explaining, shaming. Painting and drawing with unerring precision. ("You have brought that duomo too far forward," he will tell a student. Then, with a few strokes that seem effortless, almost lazy, he will correct the mistake, and the church will fall into the background where it belongs.)

But clawing at the earth? Wasting energy, looking for something he might not find? No, the idea of Prospero Fontana, portraitist to the noblest families in Bologna and Florence, commissioned by the court of France and by the Vatican, on all fours, stockings red with clay, hands rubbed raw, is too preposterous, too laughable to even consider.

Her father is giving instructions now, the temple of his hands collapsed, his arms folded. "When Catanio arrives, we will hold a banquet in his honor." His voice has assumed the clipped, peremptory tone he uses with his students. "Have the old woman bring in her grandsons. A female cook cannot handle this alone." A weary look toward Antonia, half regret, half rebuke. "I told you we should hire another man when her husband died, did I not?"

He prods the chicken in front of him with one of the pearl-handled forks he has had shipped from Sigonella and, with a tolerant, almost sorrowful smile, exiles the meat to the far side of his plate. "This gentleman is important, well connected. We must show him every courtesy." He leans for emphasis toward Vini's mother. "And that includes meals he can digest."

Antonia blinks into his sun. "I will make a list, my dear," she says. "I can get the stable boy to help with the heavy work. And I might hire those musicians who played at palazzo Aldrovandi in the spring." She pauses, as if surprised by her own audacity in volunteering this suggestion. She lowers her eyes, and Vini watches her hands begin their frightened mouse dance under the table. "That is, if you think we should spend the money?"

"Of course, of course." Prospero's tone suggests he has thought of music long before now. "And you will play one of your pretty little tunes for our guests, too." He has turned to Vini, though there is a vestige of the exasperation his wife always induces still on his face. "Won't you, Lavinia?"

She nods. "*Sì, Padre.*"

"The good father must have taught you something new, no?" His expression is lighter now, not fond, but relieved of irritation. "Something that will show Catanio Bologna does not need to dance to Florence's tune, eh?"

The priest who comes to the house every week, who brings old church music and the smell of anise with him, has, in fact, taught Vini nothing new in months. Instead, he sits behind her, watching her while she plays the same hymns over and over. The instant he hears the great public clock in the piazza ring the hour, he creaks to a standing position, sighs, and blesses her before he leaves.

No matter. Vini will get Silvana's youngest daughter to sing the tune she heard her humming over the laundry last week. Or she will ask Zia Beatrice, her aunt, to bring some new music books. "*Sì, Padre.*"

And all the time, it is the drawing she thinks of. How she still needs to get the background right, the way the scene behind the puppets looked as if it had been painted by a child, the sheep, the mountains, the stream all spread out like paste across the cloth.

Father would have hated the lack of perspective. "Remember the vanishing point," he is always telling his students. "Objects become smaller as they move toward the horizon." But clearly, the person who painted the puppet's scenery had never heard of the vanishing point. The sheep in the foreground were the same size as the ones in back, so that they seemed to be standing on each other's woolly heads!

The vanishing point, Vini thinks as her father drones on. *The place where things get so small they disappear.* Perhaps she and Mama seem that small to Prospero. She stares at him now, huge and threatening as the griffin on the rug by her bed; and at her mother, pale and helpless as the dove, worn away with the years. But this dove cannot nestle under the protective wings of the griffin. This dove has nowhere to hide her restless hands, her wide, frightened eyes.

Is this what tightens Vini's belly? What keeps her from eating more than a few mouthfuls until Silvana has taken the pewter chargers and trays away? Until, dismissed, she doubles back to the kitchen, scoops Cesare up in her arms, and walks to the table beside the hearth. Sighing, she takes a seat on the bench by the tiny trestle one quarter the size of the table she has just left. Suddenly, she feels easy, light. Glancing around the moist, familiar room, she realizes she is starved.

Chapter Four

"THE TOWER," SILVANA TELLS VINI AS SOON AS SHE SEES HER. SHE leaves the sink to stand beside the girl. Together they study the tarot deck arranged across the table. "It is the card of change." The old woman's voice is like rough-cut stone; she has so few teeth all her words run together. "Look. Look there." She points to the card in the center.

Vini strokes Cesare's ringlets, damp from the kitchen's heat, and considers the picture on the card. Two people, a man and a woman, are falling, head over heels, from a burning tower. A lightning bolt splits the sky behind them. Vini likes the design of this card, even though the doomed pair are screaming, their mouths open as if they could outyell the thunder.

It is the way their bodies are stretched, she thinks, between the earth and the sky that charms her. The rings on their fingers, the fur at their throats, the bell of the woman's dress as she floats, headfirst, toward the ground.

"I have told your mother," Silvana says now. "But she will not listen." She sets a bowl in front of the girl, ladles in the food Vini left uneaten at dinner. "The Tower is crossed by the Hanging Man. There will be darkness in this house before the year is out." She puts down the ladle and points to a second card. "Darkness and death."

Vini looks where Silvana points. The Hanging Man, too, is upside down, dangling by his feet and twisting toward the grass from a gnarled tree. But she is not frightened by this card, either; in fact, she decides to draw it. How full of drawings the world is! She settles the little dog on the bench beside her and begins to eat, but the old woman grabs her hand.

"The cards do not lie." Silvana's mother was a Gypsy and the old woman herself is a fortuneteller. Everyone knows it; dozens of ladies in town have sent their servants to the Fontana kitchen over the years. Sometimes they claim to be after figs or extra firewood or a bit of oil, but always they have a question about their mistresses' affairs, about what tomorrow holds in store.

Vini only smiles into Silvana's alarm and continues to eat. Sighing loudly, the cook picks up the cards like old friends, one by one, studying each face before she wraps it in the orange-and-green scarf where she hides the deck. "They do not lie, and they do not forget."

Vini's parents pretend to take no notice of Silvana's reputation in the neighborhood. Occasionally, though, Antonia seeks her old maid's counsel, asking offhandedly, as if she puts no stock in the answer at all, whether Silvana thinks Zia's ague will take a turn for the better, or whether the heavy rain will rot grains and drive up the cost of bread. Vini has noticed her mother's narrowed eyes when she asks these questions, has seen how carefully she studies the old woman's face.

Prospero, naturally, dismisses Silvana's predictions as nonsense. "Women's foolishness," he calls them. "Best not let this tongue-wagging reach the church, Antonia. Do you want to lose your cook to a witch's trial?"

Vini cannot believe how good this food tastes. Free from her mother's trapped mice hands and her father's pronouncements, she devours the lukewarm dinner. Even though Silvana is watching her every move, waiting for a response, she sops up the last bits of gravy with one of the seeded rolls the old woman gets up early to lay in damp rows along the kitchen window.

"I have done three readings, Preziosa." Vini has finished now, and Cesare is licking her fingers clean with his tiny rasp of a tongue. The old woman takes Vini's empty bowl as license to resume her verbal hand-wringing. "Three readings for this family." Her eyes are limpid and pale, not Gypsy eyes at all. "They are always the same." She looks at the scarf as if she could see through it to the misfortune inside. "Darkness and death."

Vini rises from her place, leaving Cesare still glued to the bench, hoping for more gravy. She sweeps the cook into a hug.

"You worry too much, Old One," she says. "I am a *maga*, too." She grins, then releases Silvana to stretch her arms across the tiny, rich-smelling room. "But I am a more powerful sorceress than your venerable self. Give me the card of the Tower, if you would be so kind."

Hesitantly, despite Vini's smile, Silvana unwraps the scarf. Her eyes are frightened as she hands over the card.

"Now then." Vini stares solemnly at the Tower, watching Silvana out of the corner of her eye. At last she grins. "Just as I thought." She turns the picture upside down and hands it back. "You see? The lady and gentleman of the house are dancing and singing for joy!"

Vini is surprised. Usually her antics amuse Silvana, but the maid only stares at the card blankly, then rights it. Once she has wrapped the Tower up with the rest of the deck, she unties a small packet from her apron.

"*Per Dio.*" For God's sake. "Take this." She pushes the packet into Vini's palm, then closes the girl's fingers around it.

Vini opens her hand and sees a stoppered vial before the old cook wraps her fingers back into place. "Keep this hidden," Silvana whispers. "It is for protection. You must cut the tips of your toenails and add them to the herbs."

Vini has seen the *ciarlatani*, the men selling magic elixirs in the street, their booming voices careening off little stages in the piazzas. "What ails you," they yell to passersby, "need not. End your suffering now." Then, when the crowd is large enough, they allow themselves to be bitten by snakes or cut by swords. When they drink their potions and rub secret oils on their arms, the wounds are miraculously healed.

"You should not spend your money on me, Silvana." Vini puts the vial in her sleeve, carries her bowl to the huge stone tub where the other dishes wait. Cesare, roused by the clatter, comes to investigate, then begs a lift up.

"On who else?" Silvana pours a pitcher of water into the tub. "Both my daughters can take care of themselves. But you"—her voice cracks with fondness, and she bats Vini's hand away from the tub—"you are too smart for your own good. Go." She pushes Vini and the dog out into the hall. "Go and cut your nails. Before it is too late. Before the Tower falls."

It is good to leave the hot kitchen, to step outside; to sit on a stone bench in the herb garden while Cesare scampers off on urgent night business across the courtyard. Vini searches the sky for the tender prints of new stars as the purple basil turns darker and darker in the fading light. She is thinking about the Hanging Man, the way he clutched at the ground, the way his body twisted like a braid, when she hears a clatter by the studio door.

Glancing up, she sees Paolo Zappi, the shop boy, on his hands and knees, gathering the dozen oranges and the two wooden bowls he has dropped. But the poor pony is so clumsy that no sooner does he have one bowl full, then he tips it over to fill the other, and the fruit is once more rolling across the courtyard tiles.

She does not mean to be rude, but the laughter comes before she thinks, merry and loud enough to make Paolo search the dusk in her direction. When one of the wayward oranges arrives near her left foot, Vini stops laughing and scoops it up. "Here, Signor Zappi," she says, walking over, stooping beside him. "Let me help."

Paolo drops three more oranges as he stands to bow. *"Grazie,"* he says. Thank you. It is hard to be certain in this half-light, but it looks as though the young man is blushing, deepening like the basil. "I was just going to set up the still life the Master wants for tomorrow." He stoops again to help her gather the fruit.

"You work for my father when others are at liberty?"

"I would do anything for him." He pauses, looks at Vini, his eyes faintly lit as the baby stars above them. "And for you, Little One," he adds.

"Paolo," she tells him, forgetting, in her frustration, to address him formally, "you are seven years older than I am, granted. But does that oblige you to constantly call me 'little'?" *I am nearly as tall as you, Sir Pony,* she thinks. *And I am able to converse without shedding fruit like a tree in autumn.*

"Why, it is merely an endearment." The Pony studies his hands and drops another orange. "That is to say," he corrects himself quickly, "I mean no harm by it, Signorina."

"Besides," Vini continues, ignoring his apology, "there is no need to thank me for helping." She stands now, her skirt full of oranges, and when Paolo rises, too, begins putting them, one by one, into the bowl he holds out. "It is small repayment for the three sheets of drawing paper you will procure for me."

"More paper? Already?" Paolo stoops for the second bowl and holds it out to her. "I just stole—er, procured some for you two days ago."

"I am working on something special, Paolo. Father will not miss a few more sheets." *He must not, he cannot.*

"I will do my best, Little One." Paolo threatens to bow again, and both bowls list perilously in his arms. Vini puts her hand on his chest to stop him. She finds herself smiling, the Hanging Man and the crumbling Tower forgotten.

"And in helping me, Sir, you are helping my father, no?"

"Perhaps, but—"

"It is not stealing, so much as taking from one member of the family and giving to another." It is remarkable how this fellow amuses her, she thinks. How he lifts her away from the griffin and the dove.

"Still, Signorina, your father—the Master—gives me a bed and food. He is training me—"

"Your parents are paying him well, and you are serving him faithfully." *A wealthy student from Imola is a feather in Father's cap. Even if you were twice as clumsy, good Pony, he would be loath to let you go.*

"I hope to prove worthy of his trust."

"And *I* hope to prove to you, my friend, how grateful I am that you are keeping our little secret."

"I am already repaid." Paolo's voice seems to tremble, but perhaps it is the exertion of crawling after oranges that leaves him breathless. "Your friendship is all the reward I require."

"But I want you to see these pages you have pilfered, Signore. I want to share what I am working on with you." Vini's own voice is eager now, tumbling over the words. "I need your opinion."

"Mine?"

"Of course. You are an artist in my father's *bottega*. You will know . . . "

"Vini? *Viene!*"

It is her mother calling. There is embroidery to do on the napkins for the banquet. Vini curtsies and, finding no place for the last orange in Paolo's heaped bowls, decides to keep it herself. "If he will not miss paper, perhaps Father will not miss an orange, eh?" She laughs, pocketing the treat for later.

"Vini?" *How is it Antonia can fill a single word with such worry, such desperate care?*

She puts her fingers to her lips. "Shhhhh! Remember, Paolo, not a word."

"On my honor, Little One." His whisper is husky, earnest. "I would never betray you."

Grateful, Vini whistles for Cesare, then races inside. So long as she will have more paper, she is content to sit for now beside her mother, to send stitches, like tiny soldiers in orderly ranks, across the bland, crisp plains of her family's linens.

Chapter Five

EVERYONE HAS BEEN INVITED TO THE FEAST IN HONOR OF THE
archaeologist Pietro Catanio. Everyone who is rich and well connected. Which means, of course, the Fontanas' guests include
Paolo and his parents. If Prospero cannot bring himself to make
the Pony an actual apprentice, he continues to humor the wealthy
Zappis, to tell them how much promise their son shows. He is
always careful around money, Vini's father.

Vini is caught off-guard by Paolo in his street clothes. He looks
taller, less clownlike in his doublet and cape. And when the Zappis
are seated at her family's table, she is not sorry to see him smiling
at her over his wine goblet. It is like having an ally, another out-
sider, in the middle of this elegant chaos.

Silvana's daughters and their seven children have spent all day
twining ivy around the pillars. And carrying benches out to the
courtyard, nesting them between the torches, hauling out every
last one of the goblets and plates. Now the bronze and silver

bowls catch the light and glow like small moons from the center of each table.

Across the courtyard, in front of the fountain, the musicians are playing a strange, sad tune, too sad for a supper under the stars. A boy, not much older than Vini, is strumming a *chitarra*. He has a gold-colored leg band and a dark curl that hangs naughtily over one eye. One of Vini's younger cousins giggles and blushes each time he looks toward their table. She is acting ridiculous, Vini thinks, calling attention to herself, but the boy only turns away, closes his eyes, and listens to his own sweet song.

Vini has been allowed to eat with adults for the last two years. But endless, silent dinners with her parents have not prepared her for this noise, this delicious confusion. When she was younger and supped with her nurse and Silvana in the kitchen, there were stories, yes. And sometimes Destina would whisper to the old cook, and they would howl with laughter. Usually, though, the single candle on the table burned steady and low, and the two women's voices were as regular as cicadas' hums, soothing Vini into a languorous stupor, then into sleep.

But tonight the blaze of light and the layers of conversation bobbing and weaving around the tables make Vini dizzy. And excited. She is part of a bigger world now, a world where people talk about art and books and the Church. A world where the eminent archaeologist stands to thank his hosts and their "lovely daughter" for their hospitality. As all the guests raise their glasses,

Vini can feel the heat flood her neck and face. She feels her own smile, too, her pleasure.

She is wearing a heavy grass-colored dress with heaps of yellow silk, like folded dough, peeking through its slashed sleeves. With the new dress, she has put on a new name. She is no longer "Vini," a name that suits a small dog like Cesare better than it does a gentlewoman of Bologna. It is a snippet of a name, fine for a puppy that needs to be locked inside during parties, that is likely to wander away unless carefully watched. "Here, Vini." "Sit, Vini." "Stay."

Tonight she is Lavinia—even to Antonia, who nods and smiles at her daughter as if she were a willow, a crystal, a natural wonder. "Lavinia has such a way with a needle," Mama says, her eyes liquid with candlelight. "Did I show you her latest tapestry? Have you ever seen such work? Me? All I do is prick my poor fingers until they bleed!"

Vini wants to remind her mother of the rug by her bed. She has heard Antonia say many times how long it took, how hard she and Vini's aunt worked to make the griffin's teeth glisten like ivory. But it is no use; Antonia will only laugh at herself. She will give all the credit to her sister, to Zia Beatrice, who talks too loudly and is always giving orders. "Monsters don't smile, silly goose!" Vini can picture her aunt leaning over her mother as they stitch: "Fiercer, darling. Much fiercer!"

For now, then, Vini is Lavinia, with a small rope of pearls twisted around her hair ribbon. Nibbling bites of peacock and eel, delicacies her father has permitted for this special occasion, she shakes her head at the whispered confidences of Ginevra. Ginevra is not like Vini's other cousins. For one thing, she is older; for another, she is more worldly. She bleaches her hair, she is engaged, and she has an exotic habit of widening her eyes when she whispers. Everything she says sounds exciting.

It is while Ginevra is quoting from memory a lovelorn endearment in the last letter from her betrothed, that Vini realizes Paolo is standing behind them. He has not said anything, but he does not need to. Vini can feel him there, waiting. How does he know she wants to talk to him? He is always close at hand, it seems. Always ready, this obedient Pony, even before she calls him.

It is just as well, since they have so little time. One more tune, perhaps two, and the cherries and cheese will be brought out. After that, her father will remember the spinet. Then he will herd everyone into the music room to listen to the song Vini has promised him. But first she must speak with Paolo. She must show him the picture.

She waits until Ginevra has finished whispering and sighing, then announces that she needs to practice. She slips from the table, and together she and Paolo cross the courtyard.

When they are past the musicians, when they can hear the chuckling of the fountain behind them, she grabs the young man's hand, a finger over her mouth. She pulls him into the dark.

"What?" Paolo, looking handsomer, less awkward in the moonlight, pulls against her. "Where are we going, Little One?"

For once Vini does not scold him about the silly nickname. Let him call her whatever he wants, so long as he goes along with her plan.

"Here," she coaxes, opening the door to the music room, shutting it quickly behind them. "I want you to see something."

Six sconces are already lit, ready for "our little musicale," as Prospero has been calling it all evening. Vini leads Paolo through the wavering shadows, through the tangle of chairs and music stands, then takes her drawing of the puppets from its hiding place. She stands beside the hearth, where the fire bathes the page in blond light.

And that is when she sees it—a look of such hunger and longing on his usually impassive face, that for a minute, she thinks Paolo may cry. "You like it?" she asks softly.

The Pony says nothing, only drinks up her drawing with his solemn, yearning eyes.

"It is the puppet theater," she tells him, trying to snap him from his trance.

"I know."

"They put on *The Duke of Mantua*." She frowns. "It is not the same thing they did last month. When do you suppose they will finish the *Adventures of Orlando*?"

Paolo does not answer her question. Without looking up from the drawing, he runs a hand through his thick hair. "I would give one of my legs to be able to make something so beautiful."

When her mother tells Vini that she is as luscious as a princess, as blessed with talent as Saint Catherine, the wisest, most precious daughter in all of Christendom, it means nothing. But this is different.

Paolo is in earnest. Vini sees it—in the way he cannot meet her eyes, in the way his voice sounds as if he is in church. This almost-man, who works so hard for her father, who laughs only when Prospero laughs, who trips and spills paint and stays to clean up while the rest of the apprentices are set free, tearing down the street in a crazy, howling mob. He knows her work is good.

She looks at the drawing with him. She has left the audience in shadow, has picked out the stage with light from the right and overhead. ("Know where the sun is," her father always tells the hares and tortoises, "and your scene will be warmed with truth.") She would need paints to get the skin tones right, the complicated mixture of hues that make painted flesh look lit from inside. ("More ochre in old skin, more rose in young.") For the puppets' faces and hands, of course, simple whites and browns would do.

"Have you shown this to the Signore?" Though his parents own a palazzo twice the size of the Fontana house, Paolo speaks of Vini's father as if he were a nobleman, a duke or prince. "What does he think?"

"Nothing yet," Vini says. "And *I* am not going to show it to him."

He turns to her, astonished, but before he can say another word she puts her finger to her lips again. When he is quiet, only those wide eyes staring, she tells him, "I want *you* to take it to him."

"Me?" Paolo is a pony again, trembling under her lead, uncertain and nervous. "What do you mean?"

"I mean, my father must take on another apprentice."

"But he will. He has already promised me." Paolo looks away again, embarrassed. He is, after all, the oldest shop boy Prospero has ever employed. "Next year I will be a full apprentice, Little One."

"I mean *now*, not later." Vini has lost her diplomatic tone, has forgotten how eager she was, only a minute ago, for the Pony's approval. "And I do not mean *you*, I mean *me*."

"You?" He stares at her as if she has blasphemed or slapped him. "An apprentice?"

"Why not?" She laughs, sounding more confident than she is. "This is Bologna, after all. There are women in the university. Why not in my father's studio?" She laughs again, then wishes she had not.

"He will not look at this if I take it to him." *Why is she talking so fast? Why are her hands so moist?* "Oh, he will look at the page, but he will not *see* the drawing."

The Pony turns back to the sheet of paper, studies it greedily.

"But if *you* show it to him, if you present it as *your* work . . ."

He looks up, astonished. "And when he finds out the truth?"

"I will explain it all," she promises. "I will tell him how I begged you, poor thing. How, when begging did not work, I forced you, tortured you." She reaches under the pleats of his cape, tickling the silk doublet, digging her fingers into his ribs.

Paolo is laughing now, backing away.

Vini stops her pursuit, tilts her head to one side. It is an angle she knows well, and the expression she shows him now is one she has practiced again and again. It is the face her mother can never resist.

"Oh, please, Paolo." Half pout, half smile. "You must do this for me. I will never ask you for anything else again." She begins to cross herself above the drawing, but he prevents her, grabbing her free hand.

"Not even to reach the first figs?" he asks. "Not even to bring you yellow chalk?"

Vini is chastened. He has kept her from lying to God. She lowers her eyes from his.

"Not even to get more of this paper?" He does not let go her hand, only nods toward the picture.

But now she has gained ground. Her fingers still swallowed in his, she senses her advantage. She raises her head, traps his eyes in hers. *"Per piacere?"* Please?

The Pony pulls his hand back and releases her. But he cannot look away. "I will think about it, Little One," he tells her solemnly. "I will consider what you ask."

Like a *padrone,* Vini thinks. Like a great lord mulling over a servant's request. In the courtyard, there is the scraping of benches, the sound of talk moving toward them. Again, her fingers are on her lips and she is pulling him through the door. *A padrone,* she smiles to herself, *who will do just what I want.*

Chapter Six

IT IS OVER SEVEN DAYS SINCE THE LEARNED DOCTOR CATANIO and Vini's father have returned from Rome, since Catanio wept and hugged Prospero, then set out for Florence, newly convinced that other city-states besides his own enlightened home contain glimmers of civilization and polish. For eight days, Papa has cleaned and fussed, installing in glass-paneled cabinets the jars and plates and the two precious busts unearthed on their expedition. But now he is finished, now it is time.

Paolo promised Vini it will be today, but he could not tell her when. So she has found a thousand excuses to go outside, to linger in the courtyard, where she can hear what happens in the studio. But she has made so many trips, from the kitchen to the herb garden, from the garden to the courtyard, and then to her hiding place under the *bottega* window, that she has gotten tired, careless.

Although she has dreamed over and over of the words Father

might use, Vini misses most of them. Perhaps she was filling the water jug at the fountain when Paolo showed him the drawing. Maybe she was cleaning Cesare's drinking bowl or watering the lavender and fennel, when the two men stood together to look at the picture in the light from the window. So now she hears only the end of a conversation she wishes she could have sucked up like one of the thirsty plants she has just fed.

"Yes. Yes, Zappi," Prospero is saying. "I did not think you had it in you, boy. But see how I was wrong."

Vini puts down the water jug and stands, frozen. She knows, the way you sometimes recognize when you are happy, that she will never forget this damp smell from the bottom of the jug, the cautious joy in her father's voice.

"Look here." *To what is he pointing? What is it that makes him sound so proud and so humbled at once?* "The seeds are here. I can take you far, *figlio.* You must move your things in today."

Their backs are to her, so she cannot see their faces. But she hears Paolo protest, hears her father ignore him. "This instant, I insist, lad. There is no time to waste." He stops, and she knows he is looking at the drawing again. They are so close to the window that his hair will cast a shadow on the page. Perhaps, this once, he will forget to brush it back.

"How did I miss the eye that caught this? And this?" *What? What is it he approves?* Another pause. "Here, of course, the light is wrong, but that is easily remedied." *Where? How?* "And here, too, there is a mistake. *It must be the duchess's dress,* Vini thinks. *She still has not gotten the folds right. But she can do better, she knows she can.*

The thrill is palpable, an unruly warmth that spreads across her chest and fills her throat, tries to force its way out in a shout. She crouches down low, makes herself stay calm as she backs away from the window, hoping to reach the garden before she bursts with excitement. Moving sideways, a happy, eyeless crab, she does not see Cesare, who, released to the courtyard, dashes joyfully toward her. She does not remember the water jug she has placed on the ground. And so she stumbles into both, sending the dog yammering back toward the house and the jug clattering across the courtyard tiles.

Scrambling after the jug, Vini trips and falls. She screams in spite of herself, in a frenzy of triumph and pain. She has twisted her ankle. Maybe it is God, she thinks, sending her a reminder in the middle of delight. You can never climb so high that He cannot bring you down. All you have, He has given you, and He can take it from you whenever He wishes.

The noise has brought them both to the window. Paolo's face is in front. Behind him, Vini's father is staring at her, too. "It seems," he says, almost laughing, unperturbed, "we have a new theme for this afternoon's painting: Fountain Nymph Felled. Eh, Paolo?"

"Are you all right, Little One?" The Pony is leaning halfway out the window now, as if he could help her up from its ledge.

Vini stands by herself. She feels her heartbeat in the swollen ankle, but she smiles, brushes off her skirt. "*Si.* Of course, only the jug . . ." She looks down at the jagged pieces of earthenware.

"Do not trouble yourself, Lavinia," her father tells her. His hand slices the air, pushes the matter behind them. "Have Silvana fetch another from the storeroom. And remember, you are a young woman now." He chuckles benevolently. "Nymphs do not run like silly children."

His head withdraws from sight. Vini knows he is anxious to get back to the world of his workshop, a consistent, precise world, where jugs are works of art, not water carriers.

"Did you hear?" Paolo asks her. "He wants me to move in. I am to be an apprentice!" He has leaned so far over the sill to whisper to her, she is afraid he will fall, too.

"I heard," she says. She has to look away from his happiness, his shining face.

"I suppose you must tell him now?" It is as if he has asked if she will wring his slender pony neck, break his pony heart.

"I am not sure."

He has started breathing again.

"I did not color the picture, Paolo." Vini is convincing herself; perhaps it *is* too early to be sure. "He might not like the way I paint."

"Paolo." The voice from inside is peremptory, no-nonsense. "I need you."

Paolo unclutches the window frame. "I have to go."

"I will do one more, a painting this time. And then, if he likes that too . . ."

"You will tell him?"

"Yes."

Paolo turns back to the window. "But won't that be worse?" he asks, suddenly sober. "The longer we wait, the angrier he will be. He may kick me out altogether." He looks bereft. "I would never see you again, Little One."

Vini is angry. Why is Paolo whining? It is *her* ankle, not his, that is throbbing.

"Paolo." The voice is painstakingly patient. Her father has not sharpened his tone at all. Perhaps this is because he so seldom calls anyone twice.

Paolo holds one finger to his lips, just as Vini did the other night in the courtyard, then his face disappears into the dark of the studio.

Vini is seized with jealousy. She pictures her father's arm around his new apprentice, strains to hear the confidences, the advice he is offering. She can almost feel Paolo's pride in her own chest, the thrill of the chosen student, the one singled out to sit with the Master.

And Vini? She must still creep and sneak and spy. She is furious—with Paolo, with herself, with all the mistakes she made in the drawing. She kicks at the shards of jar, striking out with her wounded leg. Instantly, an arrow of pain shoots from her foot to her knee. She shrieks again, sinks to the ground, and doubles up in agony.

This time they come outside, rush over to her, Paolo kneeling on the tiles, Prospero bending to put his hand on her shoulder. "What?" he asks. "What now?"

Vini cannot answer him. She is crying too hard. She has never interrupted her father's work before. She has never caused him so much trouble in one day. She tries to stand and falls back onto the tiles. Bits of the grass that struggles up between them have worked their way into her hair. Paolo picks a blade out, holds Vini's hand, then, glancing nervously at Prospero, releases it.

"Are you hurt, Lavinia?" her father asks. "Can you walk?"

Vini nods, but keeps crying. "I . . . I," she sputters through her tears. "I did not mean to break it."

"Calm yourself." Prospero has lowered his voice, but it still sounds like a command. "Paolo and I will help you up. Take my hand."

She is standing between them now, or rather, hanging between them, like one of the boneless dolls Destina used to make for her out of old dress sleeves. "Lean on me," her father urges, leading her toward the kitchen.

The pain ebbs and Vini realizes she can put weight on her foot again, but she is tempted to prolong this moment. Shyly, experimentally, she puts her head on her father's broad chest. She can hear his heart beating—under the thick leather shop apron, under the shirt beneath that, there is a heavy, regular rhythm, a sound like a large cat purring.

"Madonna!" Antonia must have seen them from the window; she is on them in seconds, hovering, cooing, soothing. *"Bambina mia!* What have you done?" She strokes her daughter's hair and loops her own frail arm through Vini's. Cesare, too, has rushed to meet them, is weaving around everyone's ankles. "We will make a poultice. I will send Silvana's girl to the apothecary."

Her father's heartbeat, the pressure of his bear's embrace vanish. He is passing Vini on to her mother, as if she were a small, forgettable problem—a torn vest, a missing spoon. "It is nothing, Antonia. Just a silly fall." His voice has turned to stone; there is no trace of concern or involvement. "Paolo and I must get back to work. We have important business, eh, *figlio?"*

He and the Pony turn on their heels, but Prospero stops after a few steps. "Daughter," he calls, then begins to walk backwards, still widening the space between them.

"Sì, Padre." Vini raises her eyes to his, hoping for nothing.

"Do not let your mother send for any of those healers she favors." He almost smiles. "Not unless you want to find yourself suffering from some smart new ailment with a costly cure." He looks to the Pony for confirmation, and when Paolo grins up at him he turns around again and walks away.

And it is while they are fussing over her, her mother and Silvana and Cesare, that Vini thinks it: *Paolo loves my father. And my father loves Paolo, as much as he can love anyone. Paolo should have been my father's son. He would not be the eighth in line, then, starving for attention. He would be the Figlio Primo, the First Son. The Prize.*

Her ankle is swelling now, and the wrap of muslin and hot mustard greens feels good. So does the sound of women's chatter, the smell of the midday meal, and the exhaustion that is creeping over her. She will take a nap instead of sneaking out today. She will stay where she belongs. And in the dreamless sleep of afternoon she will forget the picture of her father and Paolo leaving her behind.

But, of course, she cannot sleep. She has already decided what her new painting will be. Or rather, they have. For by the time she gives up trying to rest and sneaks down to the music room for her paper, Vini can see the sketch. How it will be set on the page; how the two figures, one tall and powerful, the other small-boned and angular, will seem to walk away, toward the picture's horizon. *Insieme*, she thinks. Together. *They will walk together.*

Vini finishes the drawing in minutes, perspiring in the late sun that pours through the shutters she has opened. She sketches the two men half in, half out of the shadow from the courtyard wall. She blocks in the water falling from the fountain in the foreground, closing them off with a curtain of dancing light.

When she studies it, she knows it is good. Better than the

other. But it is just the beginning. The test will come tomorrow, when she has talked Paolo into stealing some paints. She will need blue for the shadows, green and purple for the water, and yellow for the light. And beneath these, the red and brown of the terra cotta, the cream of the sky.

She will need them all, all she can get. It will take time, but Paolo will do it. He will bring her the paints and he will show her how to use them. Reluctantly, dutifully, hue by hue, he will help her start her own little studio. Where? Perhaps the gardener's shed or the storeroom. Somewhere with light, somewhere the smell will not give her away, Vini will finish the painting. The painting that will make her—not *Figlio Primo*, never that, but someone her father respects. Someone he no longer looks through, but sees, actually sees.

Her drawing is done, her ankle has stopped throbbing. But still Vini cannot sleep. Back in her room, she lies behind her drawn bed curtains, eyes open, mind racing. She tries to calm herself by reciting her Latin lesson.

That first Lavinia, the one whose grief Vini has parroted back to Signor Riggio for weeks on end, stays at home and gets the gruesome news from the battlefield, secondhand:

Then sad Lavinia rends her yellow hair
And rosy cheeks; the rest her sorrow share:
With shrieks the palace rings, and madness of despair.

The spreading rumor fills the public place:

Confusion, fear, distraction, and disgrace,

And silent shame, are seen in every face.

Confusion. Shame. And why not? That long-ago Lavinia is help-less as a child. She can only recoil at the reports of distant butcheries, war waged for her sake. She cannot lift an ax or wield a sword or hack her way to glory. Her role in the story is simply to wail and wait.

Why, Vini wonders, turning onto her belly in the heat of the afternoon, are women always waiting? At windows, as parades of men pass by in the street below; in gardens and studies and kitchens, as men paint pictures, build churches, and go to war.

Instead of making her dreamy, reciting her lesson has stirred Vini up. How can she lie here, stripes of sun creeping across her sheets through the shutters, the white fingers of a plum tree tap-ping at the window to be let in? How can she nap while Prospero is teaching Paolo about perspective? While three piazzas over, the puppeteers are opening their curtains on yet another performance? How can she sleep while a servant and a chestnut vendor are yelling at each other in the street? While Ginevra, tucked away in her *camera* off Via Castiglione, is writing an endless letter to her future husband? While somewhere, leaning against a stone bench in a dappled garden, the boy musician with the wicked curl is lazily tuning his *chitarra?*

Chapter Seven

IT IS LIKE EATING A PEACH, LIKE BITING INTO A CHICKEN LEG after you have been sick. After you have done nothing but sip wine and broth for days. The colors Paolo steals for her, the small tin cups he leaves every morning on the lowest shelf in the old gardener's shed, fill Vini up.

She makes excuse after excuse, tells countless lies, and spends more and more time in the small, abandoned cubby where Silvana's husband used to keep seedlings before he died. For weeks she has been shut away in the close, tight room with the smell of oils and the heady scent of her own sweat.

Today it is cold, and the wind is rattling the strawberry pots by the fountain, sending the spray of water first in one direction, then in the other. Vini ignores the pathetic yelps coming from the kitchen; she cannot let Cesare follow her, cannot let his barking give her away.

The shed has no place to build a fire, but Vini is more concerned with finishing her picture than with keeping warm. She has swept a tiny space clear and set a stool there, made another drawing table of old boards. Now she studies the painting where she left it to dry yesterday. She has transferred her drawing to one of the canvases Paolo has brought. She needs only to lay in the colors in a few more places. It is almost alive.

She likes the shadow, the tongue of purple she has added behind the pair of walking men, and the mist from the fountain in the foreground, each drop of water like a pearl. The drawing of her father, only partly painted, she approves, too. It is familiar, the way he gestures broadly and strides ahead, bending only slightly toward the shorter figure beside him.

But something is wrong with the way she has shown Paolo; she has made his legs too short, and his body, turned toward Prospero, does not match the full profile of his face. Then there is the shadow of Prospero's arm across the younger man's shoulder—*Where is the sun? It cannot be in two places at the same time, garzoni.*

But it is more than these things; they can be easily fixed. There is something else, something about the way Paolo moves. Or doesn't move . . .

Vini frowns now, sits down, and works without lifting her eyes from the picture. She tries a layer of chalk under Paolo's face and hands, hoping to nurse him to life, to find the gift he can bring to the painting. She adds more linseed oil, as Paolo has taught her to, managing to keep the paint moist, moving. It is like a language she has always known, this play of light and dark. She does not create the mud-colored *minestra*, the soupy porridge Paolo has warned her about. (He even showed her the dark thicket he made when he first tried to mix colors. "I know it is foolish to save such a thing," he told her shyly, rolling up the small canvas sheet and hiding it in his vest. "But it is the first painting I ever did.") Instead, her colors swell and fade just as she wants them to, like the high and low notes on the spinet.

And so long as she works on the larger figure, who moves like a stately giant, or the bricks in the courtyard, where they disappear into the touches of green that sprout between them, all goes well. It is the slender young man beside the giant who gives her problems.

There is a noise outside, a scurrying that is probably only the wind chasing its tail across the courtyard. But it is enough to make Vini look up from her work at last. She notices how far the sun's shadow has crept across the dirt floor. She sighs and stands, kicking the door to the shed open further, letting the light flood her makeshift drawing table. She steps away from the half drawing/half painting and looks at it from a distance. *Aghh! That is not Paolo. His body is stiff, as if there is no blood in it. Even with the light the chalk adds to his skin, he is like a figure on a Greek frieze, a puppet with no life of its own.*

A puppet! Her family has been to church twice since the last puppet show. Surely the troupe is back in Bologna by now. Back with a new performance, more magic. Vini works for a while longer but finds herself thinking not of how the courtyard tiles must diminish as they move toward the horizon, but of the piazza just a few streets away. Of the great city bustling under hundreds of towers, of the afternoon noises and smells that fill it, and of that tiny, glowing stage at its heart.

Soon she has torn off her apron and filled a jug of water to scrub her hands. She is careful, wiping away all the telltale blotches of paint. Except for one. She leaves a touch of greenish blue, like a peacock's eye, on her wrist. She will be able to roll up her lace cuff later and smell the color she has used on the fountain and for her father's vest. Whenever she needs to, at lessons or at the table tonight, she will be able to breathe in deeply and remember who she is. *Adesso, pintrici. Pay attention, painters. This is your life.*

Already there is a chill in the breeze. The fields at the edge of town are picked clean, leaving large tawny patches on the green hills. Soon shepherds will move their sheep down from summer pasture and blackbirds will build their nests near chimneys to keep warm. Today, though, there are more people pushing toward the stage than there have been all summer. Some have given up their midday meal to come; Vini can smell the roasted pork and oranges that vendors are hawking in the square. And something sharper, nastier, too: the scent of dung. There must be a tanner in the press of bodies around her.

Vini has a better view of the audience than she does of the

puppets onstage. Slowly, weaving through the crowd—"*Scusi, scusi, per favore*"—she manages to work herself halfway to the cleared area where the puppeteers have opened their magic cabinet. Now, unable to push any further forward, she resigns herself to standing on her toes to see the tops of the warriors' heads.

This afternoon, at last, they are presenting more adventures of Orlando and his brave knights. Already a bloody battle is under way, and Saracens' plumes clash with Crusaders' helmets in a furious blur of noise and color. Vini clasps her hands and sucks in her breath as bodies are tossed everywhere, one spilling offstage and dangling by its strings in midair.

Then she feels it. Not a sound, exactly, nothing she can see. It is only a hint, a sensation as insubstantial as the conviction that someone across a room is talking about you.

Ever since she turned off Santo Stefano, Vini has had the feeling that someone is watching her. Twice on the way to the square, in fact, she whirled around on the high platforms of her shoes, only to find herself alone in the street. But now, in the middle of all these townspeople, she feels it again; someone's eyes are on her, someone's breath is close and warm. She looks behind her, but everyone there is intent on the stage, watching the marionettes.

She turns back to the show just in time to see a silver-clad figure stride onto the stage. It is Bradamante, the female warrior, cousin of Orlando. All the scrambling and bloodshed stop when this heroine raises her sword, her armor glinting, her hair spreading from under her helmet in a yellow cloud. Her voice, of course, is not a woman's, but a whispery falsetto contrived by one of the puppeteers. "Help me," the lovely puppet sings, holding her hands out to the audience, mangling a high note. "I beseech you to lend your strong arms to our just cause."

"We are with you, my little beauty," a man beside Vini yells. Other men, too, cheer her on.

"All you who love justice," the puppet sings, "and hate wickedness."

"*Sonno qui!*" Someone answers her. "Right here!"

"Trounce these destroyers of the faith," Bradamante urges in her thin, ugly voice. "Show the unfaithful whose might is supreme."

A vendor near the stage throws a head of lettuce at the Saracen puppets. Next a squash and then an onion bounce off the helmets of infidel warriors. Soon the crowd is cheering and the vegetables are flying, tossed onto the stage as the enemies of the Cross fall, one by one.

Later, when Bradamante is giving her thanks to the audience, Vini feels it again. She whirls around, leaving the bright stage behind her to search the audience. At last she catches her shadow, sees a familiar figure fall back too late into the crowd.

For the first time since she has been coming to the puppet

theater, Vini fails to watch the puppeteers take their bows. She is too angry, too full of hurt. She dives into the packed bodies behind her and confronts her pursuer.

"How dare you, Paolo!" She has grabbed his cape and is shaking with fury. She has shared one secret with the Pony; now he has stolen another. "How long have you been following me? Have you done this before?" *Whom have you told, sly Pony? Who else knows where I go?*

"Little One." Paolo holds up a hand and backs away from her. He trips into an old woman with a basket on her head. Flushing, he bows to the woman and tries to take Vini's arm. "Listen to me, Little One. It is not what you think."

"But it *is* what I think," Vini tells him. She does not turn to help the woman pick up the laundry she has dropped. Instead, she advances on Paolo, one finger poking his chest. "I think you are no true friend. I think you are a sneak and a spy."

She sees the hurt on his face but cannot stop. "I think if you breathe a single word of this to anyone . . ."

"No, never." Paolo keeps trying to back away from her, but as he does, he takes her by the elbow and drags her after him out of the crowd. "I would never betray your trust."

"Then why?" Vini stops, refuses to move further. Ignoring the people around them, she cannot keep from yelling. "Why are you following me?"

"To keep you safe." Paolo stops, too. His glance falls from her eyes to the cobblestones at their feet. "Just yesterday, a fellow put someone's eye out in a fight on this very spot." He glances up to see Vini's reaction to this news, then rushes on. "A week ago Tuesday, my uncle's neighbor was robbed in an alley off Piazza Maggiore."

His voice drops. "It is dangerous for a woman to go out alone."

"I am not a child," Vini says stoutly, though she is disconcerted by what he has told her, by his hand tightened over the handle of a dagger in his belt.

"And I am not a spy, Little One." He stands beside her, only half a head taller than she, his expression a mix of courage and adoration. "I mean only to keep you from harm."

Vini sees it all at once, as if she has walked from shadow into sunlight, and she is humbled by the discovery. Paolo's stance, his voice, his drive to protect—they all show her what she has failed to notice before. The Pony is a man. Short but sturdy. Gentle yet strong. She has been leading a man around by the nose!

"Perhaps you meant well," she says. "But do you understand what my father would do to me if he found out about . . ."—she turns, gestures into the throng around them—". . . this?"

Paolo seems to sense a corner has been turned, that he is no longer in danger of losing her friendship. A grin, along with a hint of dimples, lightens his face. "It was a fine show, no?" he asks, steering them past the vendors at the edge of the piazza. "The little armor, those tiny shields? Did you see how perfect they were?"

Vini cannot help smiling, too. "Yes," she admits, calling back the flash, the sparkle. "Did you notice the serpents carved on the hilt of Bradamante's sword?" She laughs, taking his arm instead of resisting his lead. "Why, if someone were small enough to use those weapons, I warrant they would serve in a real battle."

"Orlando's soldiers were astounding. I forgot they were only puppets fighting, I was cheering them on!"

They turn toward the street, leaving the square. "I always forget," Vini confides. "And I am always sorry to remember."

Paolo grabs the moment like a sword. "So I am forgiven?" he asks. "My Little One will allow me to serve her again?" He stops in the street to bow. And though when he straightens, he is smiling broadly, Vini can see that his cheeks are bright as apples in the sun.

She responds in kind and curtsies low, holding her gown out behind her. "It will take only one small favor," she tells him, "to win back my goodwill." Because now she understands. Now she knows what she has been missing.

"And that would be?" He is still smiling, assuming dispensation.

Vini crosses her arms, her expression like Father Anselmo's at Christmas confession. "You must pose for my new picture," she tells him. *That will right what is wrong. That will make the smaller, thinner figure in her drawing come into its own.*

Paolo coughs, loses his composure. "You mean?" Though it

hardly seems possible, he grows redder still. "You mean pose like the models in the . . . ?"

"*Ma*, no!" When she realizes what he is asking, Vini is embarrassed, too. Her eyes drop, though she cannot help smiling just a bit. "You will be fully clothed." *But it will work, she can see that now. The way Paolo's hair is caught in the wind, the way his cape is opening, closing, breathing as he moves. There is music about him. Why hasn't she seen it until now? How will she put it into paint?*

"Well, then." He straightens, takes her arm again. "Of course." He has reassembled his world, his idea of the young girl beside him. "What is this painting of?"

"Two men," Vini tells him. She does not add that the drawing is of Paolo and her father. She does not tell him she is certain that when Prospero sees it he will know who the artist is, will realize that Paolo could not have painted it.

She refuses to let Paolo see the picture, even when he comes to pose for her the next day. Or the day after that. Or the one after that. Each afternoon, while the house sleeps, Vini does tiny charcoal sketches of her father's new favorite. Each day, after Paolo leaves, she transposes what she has learned from the sketches to the painting: the movement, the shy grace, the energy that is like a newborn colt, wobbly but beautiful.

Of course, Paolo knows exactly who the two figures are when

the painting is finished, when four days later she shows it to him. He is astonished and pleased, but he is quiet. As he studies her work, it is the same as before. He does not speak at first, just drinks and drinks. He holds his breath and does not look at her. "It is a masterwork," he says at last.

Vini sees what he sees. The two men walking in a garden, one turned to the other like a pilgrim, both loved by the sun. The water shimmering in front of them like a curtain of sheerest lace, and the wind following them, playing with the young man's hair, with the cape that cannot hide his sturdy shoulders or the slender hand that rests on the handle of his weapon, ready to serve. "No," she says. "Not a masterwork. A work that needs the touches a master can bring to it."

"But . . ."

"I want you to take this to my father. I want you to ask him." She knows Paolo will protest, and she knows he will do it at last.

He lifts his gaze from the painting. He looks at her with the old hunger, the hopelessness of an exile. "Ask him what?"

Vini does not look at his face, sees nothing but the picture. *There, by the fountain, that stone is not right. And the wall behind the men, it is much too large.*

"Ask him what, Little One?" Paolo repeats.

Vini turns to him. Stares at him as if he is a stupid child. "Why, how to make it better, of course."

And then she is lost again: *Here, where the taller man's hand swings back, the light is wrong. How could she have missed that? And on top, where she has let the sun break through, those clouds look like a hedgerow, not God's breath. Where is the glory? Where is the fire?*

Chapter Eight

PAOLO HAS TAKEN HER PAINTING AWAY. WITHOUT IT, THE LITTLE
shed is too shabby and lonely to bear. Vini slides the metal bolt into
place, locking the door. She is headed to the main house when she
hears a laugh. It is a sound she remembers, the sound of a cherub
in God's lap. She follows it to the stable. But when she peeks inside,
there is only Giorgio the groom, snoring on a mound of hay,
Father's Spanish stallion nibbling at his hair. She walks behind the
stable, but sees nothing except the crumbling stone wall that marks
the remains of a flower garden the old gardener used to keep.

She is turning away when the laugh comes again. And a voice
with it. "You little devil," someone says, low as a purr. "Who has
ever heard of a dog eating flowers?"

Vini knows the voice that goes with that laugh. Remembers it
from years ago when she was small, when her mother and she
would string old sheets across two chests to make a house for her
dolls. *What good children you have, Vini! See how quiet they are!* She stands still,

listens. The laugh is coming from behind the wall. Vini pushes open the battered wooden door and there, lying in the grass beside a lush terraced garden, are Antonia and Cesare.

Her mother does not see her, and Vini cannot bring herself to say a word. Who is this woman who laughs like a child? Who has woven the stems of cornflowers into a tiara for their dog? Some part of Vini, perhaps the part that has not forgotten a single one of her dolls' names, would like to make this moment last, would like to stand here forever, watching these two.

But suddenly Cesare looks up, yelps with pleasure, then leaps over Antonia's legs to bound toward Vini. And now everything is changed; her mother stops tickling the dog's nose, tosses aside the shaggy, tattered iris they have been playing with. She pushes herself to a sitting position, still flushed with a secret pleasure.

"I thought you were practicing your music," Mama says, smoothing her skirts, emptying them of grass. "I was just giving Cesare his afternoon walk." She stands now. "Your father has made it clear there can be no more . . . indiscretions."

Cesare apparently feels little guilt over the urine-soaked tablecloth one of Silvana's daughters found in the laundry basket yesterday. Or the stain on the rug in the hallway of the elegant second floor, where Prospero receives his wealthiest clients. The tiny dog's crown has been dislodged by his rush into Vini's arms. The cornflowers are draped rakishly over one eye, like the hat of a French bachelor. He licks Vini's cheek, then her nose.

"And I thought *you* were helping Silvana to sort the linens." Vini cannot keep the surprise, the scold out of her voice. She left one mother in the house, but has found a different one here.

"I was." Antonia laughs in apology. It is not the laugh Vini heard a minute ago; it is a thin, shy giggle. "But the sun began to tease me." She brushes her hair, picks up the bonnet she has left on the ground. "Imagine! It spilled right through the window and began to kiss my hand!" She glances at Vini, then at Cesare, snuggled against the girl's chest. "Besides, our little boy was begging to go out."

Vini looks over the dog's curly head at the garden behind her mother. Here, where no one would dream of looking, is splendor: pink phlox, purple sage, and Our Lady's mantle with golden flowers like perfect stars tumble down three stone terraces. Here and there, cornflowers, Madonna lilies, and irises rise above the rest. And, of course, the roses. They are everywhere, in lemon and apricot, plum and flaming red. Even this late in the year, they are nodding their full, bright heads.

"Who takes care of all this?" Now that old Umberto is dead, Vini cannot imagine anyone else working with such flowers. Her father, she knows, prefers the new style of garden , with manicured hedges and sculpture. "If you want posies for the table," Prospero has told Antonia, "have them bought at market."

"It is my little secret," her mother says. "Besides," she adds, a note of pride creeping into her voice, "I save money this way."

"And the tools?" Vini has seen no shovels, no trowels or rakes in the shed. For nearly a week she has painted there without interruption. No one has come near.

"All of Umberto's rakes and spades were sold to a peddler," Antonia tells her. "But I make do with things from the kitchen." Another giggle. A bashful smile. "Four seeds down every skewer hole. You would be surprised how fast the sowing goes!"

Vini looks again at the profusion, the glorious colors around her. It must have taken hours, days, months. Again, this woman before her seems a stranger. Pale as always, like one of her lilies, but happier than Vini has ever seen her. "Here, Mama," she says, setting Cesare down and reaching for the bonnet in her mother's hand. "Put this on."

Antonia closes her eyes and stands still, her head raised for the bonnet. Instead of tying the hat on her mother, Vini studies the life-size doll in front of her. "I am afraid La Signora Fontana has forgotten herself," she says, unable to keep from smiling.

Her mother opens her eyes, startled. Carefully, yes, tenderly, Vini removes the white rose from behind Antonia's ear. "Father will swear you have joined a band of Gypsies if you wear this to supper."

Vini hands the rose to Antonia, who holds the flower to her nose, takes a deep breath, then tucks it under the sleeve of her gown. Now, in the very same place Vini has painted her own wrist turquoise, her mother's rose hides under a lace cuff.

Vini is tying Antonia's bonnet ribbons, when they hear a low growl behind them. Both of them turn to find Cesare, who has lost his crown, straddling the blue flowers, pulling them apart with his teeth.

"*Andiamo!* Come on, little boy," Antonia calls fondly. "It is time to get out of the sun."

Vini is crouching and sneaking again. She loiters near the workshop, hoping to hear her father's reaction to the painting she handed over to Paolo. This time she has made sure Cesare is secured in the kitchen, and this time she takes no jug, nothing she can shatter in her joy. But Paolo and Prospero are at the other end of the huge room, and she cannot hear a word they say. She must settle for watching them as she walks by time and time again—forcing herself not to linger, assuming only the mild, passing interest of someone who just happens to find herself beside open shutters.

It is not until later, after supper, that Paolo is able to meet her in the music room. She has told her parents she is practicing, and practice she will. She begins playing another one of her nonsense tunes, as if to accompany his report. "Tell me every word!"

Paolo places the new painting on the spinet. "Your father says I have produced nothing like this in the whole year I have been with him." He glances at Vini's fingers as they scramble over the keys. "He says this is my finest work yet."

Vini pauses for an instant, then continues playing. *The finest yet!* She tries to hear her father saying it: *Your finest work.* They have already taken root, those words. They are growing in her heart, three dark roses with velvet petals.

"He said he has never seen such improvement, such a gift for color."

Deeper, more substantial than the white rose behind her mother's ear. *It is me, Father. It is me you are looking at.* Music bubbles up like a crazy spring from the keys.

"He wants me—*you* to work on the same subject with a different vanishing point."

"Yes." Vini nods, keeps playing. She does not look at the keys, stares only at the painting. "That would fix the shadow." *Of course.* The tune she is playing flickers like the shadow she sees in her mind, then breaks away into a dizzy, triumphant march. *The light would change then. Father has put the sun in its place!*

"He says I must—*you* must get closer," Paolo tells her. "You must fill up the frame with the figures."

The figures. "Did he know the subject of my painting, Paolo?" She pauses for a few seconds, her hands arched over the keys. "Did he guess who the two men are?"

Paolo shakes his head, looks at the colored canvas. "No, I do not think so, Little One. He said that I—*you* must have studied the two shepherds in his painting for the Bardoni family."

"But it is our own courtyard!" Vini stops playing entirely,

points to the painting, too. "Here is our fountain. Here, the door to the kitchen. There is the stairway . . ."

"*Il Maestro* does not look at work that way. He does not see a house or a body or a door. He sees art."

Vini begins to play again, banging the keys much harder than she needs to. *He sees art. But he does not see me.*

"There is more," Paolo tells her over the sharp, crisp notes. He pauses, but Vini's fingers do not. "Why are you playing while I talk, Little One?" he asks finally. "It makes it very hard to remember."

"My parents believe I am practicing," she tells the Pony, sweeping down to the lowest note she can find. "You would not have me lie to them, would you?" In truth, she cannot sit still. The excitement, the greedy longing she has contained for weeks, and now the disappointment—everything is spilling out of her, playing its own song. She was so sure her father would know Paolo could never have painted like this. *How can you not see me, Papa? I am right here!*

"There is more," Paolo repeats. He lays his hands over hers on the keys. "Much more to tell."

Vini takes her eyes from the painting for the first time. She looks at him. "What is left?"

"Your father gave me this." Paolo removes a scroll from the cape he has thrown onto an oak chest. He unrolls a blank canvas, which is overlaid with squares. He places it beside Vini's painting. "Do you see where you have put in those trees, behind the courtyard?" He points; Vini nods.

"And the bird in the sky?" She nods again.

"He wants you to paint just that part on this canvas. You must trace smaller squares on your work first, exactly four times smaller." He is still holding her hands captive. "I will show you how. What you paint will be much larger, but it will keep the same scale." He pauses until she looks at him again. "Do you know why the Master wants this done, Little One?"

"No."

"He intends to use your work as part of the background in the altarpiece for San Miguele."

"In Florence?"

"*Si,* Little One." Paolo takes his hands away, and Vini's own fly to her face.

"No!"

"Yes. Yes." The Pony is smiling. He looks as happy as if it is really he who will help with the biggest commission in the workshop, the piece her father has fussed and worried about for months. "Yes!"

Too much has happened. Too little has happened. It is coming too fast. It is coming too slowly. Vini feels the tears start, covers her face with her hands. "He did not see what I painted," she sobs. "He did not see it at all."

"But he did," Paolo tells her. "He loves it. Did you not hear?"

"The corner." She glares at him, chokes the words through her sobs. "He loves the top right corner."

Slowly, slowly, as if he is drawn to do it against his will, Paolo reaches toward her. It is enough to make her stop crying, to make her sit still, trembling but quiet, while he tucks a strand of her hair back into its velvet cap.

"I thought he would know." Her voice is a whisper now, and Paolo must lean close to hear her. "I thought he would see."

"You will tell him," Paolo says. "You will explain it all to him." Less certain, softly. "He will understand."

"It is all I want. All I have ever dreamed of."

Paolo stiffens, straightens. "I know."

Vini waits for him to say more. He has always understood how she feels. Surely he feels the same way. Surely he wants to paint as much as she. There is no sound at all in the small room.

Then, while she is listening to the silence and waiting for him to speak, Paolo does something astonishing. He leans over and puts his lips on hers. Vini sees his face lowering toward her, but because she cannot believe this is her first kiss, she does nothing to help or hinder it. She simply sits, and feels the warmth of his mouth on her own.

Kissing is not at all as cousin Ginevra has described it. Vini's heart does not leap in her chest. She does not feel like swooning or sighing or closing her eyes. Instead, she offers her lips again, studying carefully this time what Paolo does, how he looks.

His eyes are closed, she observes, and she can see the small violet veins in his eyelids, his rust-colored lashes. There is a red down on his upper lip, and a small mole by his nose. And when his mouth touches hers, what does it feel like? She will have to close her eyes, she decides, to tell.

Silvana says cooked egg yolks and sugar are not fit to drink until the top has a skin on it like cream. That is how Paolo's lips feel. And how do they taste? Vini is wondering about that when he pulls away.

"Forgive me, Little One," he says. He reties the canvas, gathers his cape. "I must beg your forgiveness."

"Forgiveness? For what?" Perhaps every kiss is different? She does not want to faint as Ginevra did. But she *would* like to try it again.

"For forcing my attentions on you. For taking advantage of your trust in me."

The wiry, glistening curls above his forehead remind Vini of Cesare's. Does his mouth taste like flowers?

"And the trust of your father. Of your family, who have always been friends with mine." He hands her the painting, out of words, ashamed.

"No." He is opening the door when Vini stops him. She sees him turn, his whole body tense, alert for the slightest signal that he should walk back. "It is I who should apologize," she tells him. "It is I who beg forgiveness."

He does not speak. But he closes the door and comes to stand beside her.

"I have asked you to lie and sneak," she says. *Poor Pony,* she thinks. *Poor sweet Pony.* "I have loaded you down with secrets." She closes the small distance between them, the painting wrapped in her arms. "And now I am going to ask you to keep one more."

He looks at her, sweet Pony, ready to carry, ready to pull, ready to serve. He looks at her and that is when, careful not to crush the picture scrolled between them, Vini kisses him again.

Chapter Nine

THE BOOK IS OLD, MUCH OLDER THAN THE ONES VINI AND HER tutors use. Mama's father was a printer, and the house is full of modern books, their leather covers in bright colors, their pages creamy and thick. But the volume her father has given Paolo to study is different. Its pages are parchment, so thin Vini can see the words on the other side when she holds them to the light. Their edges are gold, and bright specks fly off if she turns them too quickly.

But after the first time, she is careful. She opens each page slowly, full of awe, honored to hold such a thing in her lap. It is almost as if she is holding someone's hand, someone who worked day after day, writing these elegant letters, drawing these magnificent figures. And the smell! Ink, gold leaf, dust, and something stronger, more mysterious. Vini imagines it is the scent of everyone who has opened this book before her.

"I am not sure I should show you this, Little One." Paolo is nervous, constantly getting up to peer through a chink in the stone wall of Antonia's garden. "The Master gave it to me because I need to study anatomy. He said I do not seem to know how people walk or move."

He comes back to sit beside her, and Vini smiles up at him. For a few heartbeats she sees his worried face, the fading flowers behind him. For a moment she feels the fall sun on her skin and hears the low, drunken drone of late bees in the lavender. "Yes," she says. "I know."

Then she is drawn back to the book, poring over the pages. It is all so clear now. The leggings, the capes, the shirts she has painted—no wonder none of them looked right. The bodies underneath were all wrong! *Look at this joint! See how it bends! And this muscle! It explains everything.*

"If your father found out . . ." Paolo does not look at the book or even at Vini.

"My father is taking measurements in Florence." She sounds irritated, she knows, but he has made her look up from the book again. "He will not be back for two whole days." *And here. The way this leg rotates!*

"Women are not allowed to study unclothed models. It is a sin."

Vini closes the book carefully, rests one hand on the cover as if she is afraid he will try to take it from her. "How else am I to learn, eh?" She cocks her head to one side, uses the smile she reserves for such moments. "Perhaps you could draw loincloths and nightshirts on these shameless gentlemen and ladies?"

"This is not a matter for joking." Paolo sits beside her on the grass, looks earnestly into her eyes. "It is said the Pope himself once ordered a painting of Saint Sebastian's agony removed from a chapel in Siena." He pulls a patch of clover from the ground, throws some at his feet. "It seems the ladies in church confessed they had lustful thoughts about the naked martyr."

Vini laughs, opens the book, and points to a diagram. "Do you think this good fellow could inspire such thoughts in me?"

Paolo studies the figure, whose muscles and organs are drawn in red ink. He shakes his head. "It does not matter what I think, Little One," he says. "It is your father who entrusted this book to me."

"Not to you." Vini stands now, the anatomy text cradled in her arms like a baby. "He meant it for the person who did the paintings you brought him."

"Yes." Paolo follows her to the door in the wall. "And he has asked that person for more and more. Every day he calls on me for something else." He throws away the last few clover stems he has carried with him. "Something else I cannot give him."

"What do you mean?"

Paolo flushes. "The Master wants me to do drawings, studies for the others. He is treating me like one of them. No," he corrects himself, "he is treating me like the best of them."

"But that is what you wanted, no?" She comes closer, turns her back to the garden door, forcing him to face her.

"It is too hard, Little One. It is not the way I thought it would be." He shakes his head again. "Each time he calls my name, I wish I could hide. Each time he asks me to sketch in an arm or draw a tree, I do the best I can. But he always looks disappointed. Do you know that way he has?"

Vini knows.

"But then he makes the best of it, he pats my shoulder and tells me I am merely having a bad day." Paolo steps back, looks away. "Every day is a bad day. I cannot give him what he wants."

Vini stoops, careful not to let the book slip, and plucks a flower from the bottom terrace. All the blooms are losing their brightness; this may be the last lily of the season. "Paolito," she says, testing this name. His eyes turn tender, and she knows it pleases him. "Paolito," she says again, "I will try to find the right time when my father comes back. I will tell him the truth." Guilty, seeking absolution, she hands him the lily. "I promise you this."

At first, he takes her offering without glancing at it. Instead he looks at her, almost sternly. "It is the only way, Little One." But then, just as Antonia did with her rose, he lifts the flower to his nose. He breathes in and smiles.

Vini is surprised at how glad she is to see Paolo a little more cheerful at last. Earlier she had hoped her mother's garden, even faded by fall, would seem as magic to him as it does to her. She had hoped . . . but then he showed her the book and she forgot all hopes but one.

"I will keep this flower," Paolo tells her, "in token of your pledge, fair damsel." He bows like an affected courtier, making flourishes with his free hand.

Vini laughs, remembering their stolen puppet show. She makes the same deep curtsy she did in the street that sunny, wind-blown day.

She turns to leave the garden, relieved that things are easy again between them. The old door is so weathered that its wood is peeling off in strips, like the bark of a sycamore tree. As she touches it, a splinter pierces her skin. "Ai!" Vini pulls her hand away as if she has been burnt and sucks her finger. Tears well in her eyes.

Paolo unbends himself from his comic bow and comes close. "My poor damsel." Carefully, as if it might shatter in his grasp, he takes her hand in his. He inspects the injured finger, touching it softly, and then, their courtly game forgotten, he is staring at her. "My Little One." His voice is husky and fond, his eyes misted with something he cannot say.

Before Vini knows how it has happened, her finger is in Paolo's mouth and his lips are pulling on it with a tender pressure that feels as though he is drawing her out of her own body. Her knees weaken and she leans against the door, still gripping the precious book. *Ginevra*, she thinks. *Ginevra was right.* And then, *How can I ever call him Pony again?*

"Whoa now! Hold it right there!"

The call comes from the other side of the door. Paolo lets go Vini's hand and the two of them shrink against the wall, hot and ashamed.

"Easy, old man. Easy there." Giorgio's voice is softer now, cajoling. The horse he has just yelled at must have settled. "Let me get the harness off, old man. We will hang it up and get you to bed." There is a muffled snort, the sound of horse's breath, and nervous hooves. "There you go." Wooing. Caressing. "There you go."

Perhaps they should laugh, the two of them. When the groom and the horse are safely inside the stables, Vini and Paolo should whisper and giggle and maybe even try a real kiss. But Vini has learned something about kissing today. Something that leaves her more frightened than curious.

She waits quietly while Paolo opens the door a crack, peers out and then stands aside to let her through. By the kitchen garden, he apologizes for his boldness. In the courtyard, he begs her forgiveness. At the fountain, she gives it. Then, with nothing more than a few whispered words, they part.

Vini hides her book under her shawl and carries it to her room. She is glad Prospero is traveling, glad she does not have to face her parents at supper. She is just settling onto her bed with the anatomy text and a heart full of questions when Silvana knocks on her door.

"There you are, Preziosa," the cook says as soon as she is inside the room. "I have rabbit and bread pudding for you." Her bristly voice is as calming as a rough old blanket, a reminder that Vini is young yet, that love and fainting can wait. *What if Giorgio had not stopped them just now? Would Vini be mooning and sighing her life away like Ginevra?*

"You are an old dear," Vini tells her. "Rabbit sounds delicious." *Has she eaten today? Has she tasted anything but muscles and nerves and Paolo's kiss?*

"With onions and new peas." Silvana comes close, notices Vini's book. "That looks like Mr. Death, that one," she says, nodding toward a skeleton with meticulous folds of violet and green tendons attached to its bones.

Vini laughs. "That is what you and I look like under our skins, Signora." She picks up Silvana's hand, spreads out the gnarled fingers beside the drawing. "See?"

"Why would you want to know this, Preziosa?" The cook takes her hand off the page and waves it in front of Vini's face. "Me? I prefer to keep my skin on until the maggots tear if off." She heads toward the door. "Up with you, now. Your mama wants you to eat with her in her rooms. I have set a table there."

When the door is closed and Silvana's ginger and garlic smell is gone from the room, Vini is puzzled. Usually, when her father is away or dining with his apprentices in the studio, Antonia takes supper in her room alone. And now that she has stumbled on her second, secret mother, Vini can guess why.

Vini herself has always loved the times without the fancy, imported manners, the impossible standards Prospero brings to even the simplest of meals. She has counted like blessed beads the nights she is spared her father's icy chill, her mother's moist sheep eyes.

But why, then, does Antonia want company tonight? Why isn't she content to shut herself away from demands and accusations and, yes, from a daughter who gives her so little? Vini doesn't worry over this mystery for long, though, because there is a larger one waiting in the apartment across the hall. Which mother, she wonders, will she find there? The one who has hidden pleasures, a sun-splashed laugh? Or the one who lives for Prospero's nods and Vini's smile?

Antonia looks up when Vini knocks and then walks into the back bedroom. "Ah, Vini. You've come at last." Her mother sits with Cesare on her lap. She has taken off her overgown, and her hair is loose and flowing. The little dog greets their visitor with a joyful yip and, restrained by Antonia's hand on his jeweled collar, trembles with anticipation as Vini comes toward them.

"Ciao, Mama." Vini kneels beside them, nuzzling noses with Cesare. Antonia strokes her hair, and for once Vini feels no impatient urge to pull away. For a few seconds, she forgets to worry over kisses or the way joints bend; she is a little girl again. She lets her head rest against her mother's skirts and studies the room: the canvas walls painted in stripes, the tapestries and bright-faced mirrors, the spindle and embroidery frame. They have always seemed a little frivolous to her, less substantial than the hard, sharp-edged world of the studio. But why has she never noticed how cheerful it is here? How much warmer it seems than the rest of the house?

"Come," Antonia says, and the stroking stops. "Look where I have had Silvana set our table." She walks toward the broad window seat cut out of the wall. "It will be almost like an outdoor feast if we open the shutters."

Indeed, the old cook has laid out their rich-smelling supper on a table that runs the length of the large window. Vini helps her mother fold back the shutters and they settle in shawls, side by side, their backs to the night.

This meal is nothing like dining downstairs. For one thing, Prospero would never allow his wife or daughter to come to the table without a gown. He is forever praising the somber colors and high collars of the new Spanish style. If he could see Antonia's hair wild and long, the shining thicket that it is right now, he would undoubtedly smile his offended smile and deliver the lecture on decorum Vini knows all too well.

But for tonight, she and Mama wear what they wish, talk about anything they want. No speeches, no derision, no unfavorable comparisons between their family and other, more efficient, more noble homes. So it seems as if Antonia has been storing it up, all the gossip, the foolish nonsense she spills into her daughter's ears.

Starving, Vini relishes the rabbit stew, the sweet pudding cooked in almond milk. And as she eats, she nods her head, turning her mother's gossip into a mild song, a wren's trill to which she only half listens: the new stitching pattern Zia has learned from her German visitor; the goat kid that knocked over three stalls at Friday's market; the catechism school for poor children started by Father Anselmo; an alfalfa poultice Silvana swears will make baby boys.

"And do you know what?" Antonia has hardly eaten a bite. She is too busy chattering, waving her hands in the excited patterns father has warned her about more than once. "It is rude to make so much of your feelings," he tells her. "People of degree are temperate."

"It is either those hideous, runny packs," Mama says, "or my prayers to Saint Margaret, but something has finally worked!"

Vini is expected to respond, she knows, but she cannot tell how. Her mother's eyes, her reckless hands—what do they want? "Saint Margaret?" She remembers the ancient story of a chaste shepherdess whose cross got stuck in a dragon's throat. "You are praying to Saint Margaret?"

"Naturally, I have prayed before." Antonia stoops to give Cesare a piece of bread from the pudding. The dog takes it to a corner, as if he is afraid she will change her mind. "But I have never used those steaming poultices night after night." She laughs. "Perhaps Margaret was only waiting for me to help myself."

"Help yourself?"

"Vini, my love." Her mother is nearly as young-looking, as happy, as the day Vini stumbled on her in the garden. "Mother Mary has blessed me. Margaret has blessed me. Our dear Lord has seen fit to grace me again after all this time."

Vini still does not understand, is looking at her with an amused half smile, so Antonia takes her daughter's hands in hers and says it as slowly, as clearly as she can: "I am with child. I am going to give your father a son at last."

Chapter Ten

THE BABY KEEPS HER AWAKE. EVEN WHEN SHE SHUTS POOR Cesare out of her room and buries her head under both pillow and bolster, Vini can see her brother. She pictures the child her mother might have, his small hands, his tiny face. She is both elated and horrified by his possibility, by the shadow of his future falling across hers.

Mama seems so sure this child will be healthy and male. What if she is right? What if Vini were to have a little brother, like the three Ginevra has? What if he were to cling to her hand and follow her everywhere? She could take him on her lap and play the games she plays with her littlest cousins when they come to visit with Zia. She could hide her face behind her hands and tease him. *Where is Vini? Where did she go?* Then take her hands away, roll him over, tickle his tummy, and cover his own eyes. *Where are you? Where is . . . ?*

What would his name be, her brother? Would her father want him christened Prospero? *Figlio Primo,* second born but first son.

First forever in the eyes of his father. And what would a daughter with some talent mean then? *Where is Vini? Where did she go?*

That first night, when Antonia told her about the baby, Vini had let her mother's happiness carry them both along, sweep them up like a sweet, wide river and rush them ahead.

"Won't your father be pleased?" Mama had asked. "He is a gifted man, Prospero Fontana. His every move is a work of art. The good Lord has given him all blessings." She had lowered her eyes, stood up suddenly from their makeshift banquet table. "All blessings but one." She had turned toward Vini, her eyes bright with tears, her hands held tight together as if they might fly apart for joy. "But now things will be different."

Antonia had paced up and down the room, touching this and that as she talked, like someone sleepwalking, someone who needed to make sure the world was still there. "Your father is busy. His life is his work, the studio. But it was not always like that." She had stared straight ahead at something faraway. "When we were younger, he would look at me and run his fingers over the bones in my cheeks. '*Buono,*' he would say. Good." She had glanced at Vini, then, as if she'd just woken from a trance. She had smiled, waved her hands, dismissing foolishness. "But that was long ago."

Now Vini has spent two days pouring over the new anatomy book and two nights worrying about the future. Sleepless and exhausted, she has begged to skip tonight's supper and gone to bed early. Her mother, of course, insisted Silvana must bring her a light meal, but the church bells have rung twice since then. Vini assumes the old woman has forgotten. Which is just as well, she decides, settling under the sheets, too tired to undress. She would probably be too tired to lift a spoon, too. She hopes she is also too tired to think about baby brothers or human bodies or Paolo's eyes. *Paolo's eyes, which shut as he leaned over her hand, just as his lips touched her skin . . .*

She is in that slow and luscious fall that happens before sleep when she hears the knock on her door. Groggy, she remembers Silvana and supper. *"Si,"* she calls. "Bring it in."

But it is not Silvana who opens the door. It is her father. He has knocked and entered all in one clean stroke. "What is this I hear about your not eating tonight? *"Andiamo,"* he says, hurry now. "I expect you to join your mother and me at the table. I have come home with news."

News. Vini rouses herself. *Father is home early. Or late,* she thinks, returning from the lip of her dream. *It is suppertime. He is back from Florence.* She throws open the bed curtains. It must be about the commission. There will be visitors. Helpers to be hired. *"Si, Padre."* She stands, glad she was too exhausted to take off her clothes when she lay down. "I will come right away."

"We are to have houseguests next week." He seems buoyant, almost eager. "Important ones."

They are always important. Only important people are Papa's guests. "Si. Vengo." I am coming.

Prospero turns to go, then stops by the door. "You need a painting here." He studies the wall above her mirror. "Perhaps that little Holy Family? The sketch for my Medici piece?" He stands, rubbing his perfectly trimmed beard. "Yes," he decides before Vini can answer. "It is in the shop. I will bring it with me tomorrow after the noon meal."

"Thank you, Father."

"Fine, then. See you downstairs, Lavinia. And make sure . . ." He pauses, stares at something on the chest under the mirror. "What is this?" He picks up the book, leafs through it, his face darkening with each turn of a page. "What is this?" he repeats, holding the text high for Vini to see.

The slow, underwater heaviness is gone. Her muscles tighten as if something enormous is hurtling toward her. "I . . ." She needs time to think. But there is not even time to pray. "I want to learn how to . . ."

"I gave this book to Zappi before I left." His eyes are narrowed, his jaw like stone. "I put it in his hands."

"I know, Father. I—"

"Where is he?" Now her father is racing around the room. He flings the bed curtains apart, tears open the chests, and then runs to the back door, peering down the stairs that lead to the linen closet. "When I get my hands on him." He storms back to Vini. "And you! Have you no decency?" He grabs her by the arm, forces her to face him. She loses her balance and falls against him. He yanks her back to arm's length, his face contorted, hideous in its fury. "Have you no shame?"

"*Padre. Speta.*" Wait. "I can explain!"

"I trusted that little weasel." Prospero is shaking his daughter now, growling through clenched teeth. "I trusted you."

"Paolo has not been here." She gasps for breath in the second he releases her to catch his own. "He gave the book to me—"

"When? Why?" He is not looking at her; his eyes still scour around the room, searching, searching.

"Because it was meant for me." She is sobbing now, writhing in his grip. "It was meant for me, Papa."

"You?" He finally looks at her, then laughs scornfully. "What nonsense are you spouting?"

Where does she start? How does she tell him something he will never believe? "I did the drawing of the puppets, father." No sobs now, just long, trembling sighs between her words. "I did the painting of you and—of the two men in the garden."

"Don't be ridiculous." He drags her toward the door. "We will have this out right now." He picks up the book with one hand, holds his daughter in tow with the other. Vini is pulled out the door, tripping helplessly down the stairs, and hauled past her mother who comes running after them.

"What is it? What is wrong?" Antonia follows the two of them out of the house and into the courtyard.

"Papa. Please, Papa!" Vini pulls against him as he strides toward the shop. The apprentices are eating in the studio tonight. Silvana's Betta and her husband have just brought the food from the kitchen and are serving the young men from a huge pot as Prospero opens the door.

"Zappi!" It is a bark, a howl, the cry of a wild beast whose territory has been challenged. Paolo rushes out, a napkin tucked in his belt. Others come into the courtyard behind him. But Prospero apparently sees only Paolo.

"How did my daughter come by this book?" He waves the anatomy text in Paolo's face and Vini watches the boy's expression change from alarm to anguish. When he looks at her, she wills herself not to cry. "Well?"

"You said the painting needed work, Master." Paolo is stammering, desperate. He continues to look at Vini, and that is when she realizes he is not afraid for himself, but for her.

"I told Papa I did the drawing," she says. "And the painting. I told him, but he does not believe me."

"It is true," Paolo's voice is stronger, surer, as if he has only been waiting for permission to tell the truth. "The work is not mine, Signore."

Prospero shakes off his daughter's hand and she nearly collapses against him again. "What did you say?" He turns on the two of them now, as though he needs to watch them speak the words. "What did you say?"

It is so quiet that the fountain on the other side of the courtyard thunders like a torrent. Someone upstairs in the main house laughs, a distant, unintelligible sound, exotic as a bird call.

Vini cannot look at Prospero. How she hates the way her eyes, like her mother's, hide from his face. A single sob, like a hiccup, escapes, then she breathes deep and says it one last time: "I did the drawing, Father. I asked Paolo to show it to you because . . ."

"That was not your work?" Prospero has pinned the boy with his eyes and his hands, grabbing his arm now instead of Vini's. "You lied to me?"

Paolo does not step away. He stands rigid, and Vini can see her father's hands dig into the boy's sleeves, press into his slender arms.

"But, Signore, I never told you I did the drawing." His voice breaks, loses its sureness. "I merely said I wanted to bring you work that needed correction. Those pictures are better than I could ever do. You know that, Signore."

And now Prospero looks at Vini. "You," he says. It is not a question but an accusation. "How?" The two worlds, the worlds he has always kept separate, have collided. Vini reads the shock of the explosion in his eyes. It is as if he has never seen her before. It as if she is one of the clay models or a piece of cloth he has draped for his apprentices. But the clay has turned to him and spoken. The cloth has shaken itself and wrapped its armless folds around him. He has discovered her.

"I want to paint," she tells him softly, as if she, too, is at confession. The world of the kitchen and the table, of skirts that rustle and voices that rise. The world of the *bottega*, of sweat and linseed oil and tiny crystals that catch light to shine it on paper. Stepping from one to the other, she thinks, must be like walking from spotted woods into the sun. "I want you to teach me how."

"I thought it was Paolo." Her father shakes his head. "That painting. It was the paper I gave him. It was—"

"I begged him for the paper." She will not look away this time. She will meet his gaze; she will mark this moment, for good or bad. *Oh, Mother of God, let it be for good.* "And the pencils. And the paints and ink, too."

Again the stare. As if he is memorizing her contours, her shape. As if he plans to turn back to the studio and set it all down in a sketch. "It was your hand?" he asks. "And no other?"

She nods. "Paolo is not to blame."

"He has not been with you?" Her father is clearly wrestling with how to say what he wants. "Alone?" he adds.

Now it is Vini who searches Paolo's face. In the speck of time, the instant that passes before she speaks, she sees it all. The boy's permission is total. She may do whatever she wants; he will not judge her. "No," she tells Prospero. "We have not been together." The shed, the garden, those meetings were not what her father means. Blessed Mary spare her, she has told a lie that is the truth.

Prospero lets the boy's arm go, turns as if he is finally aware of the others—the shop boys, the apprentices, the servants, who have left their meal and are watching intently, some from the studio window and door, a few from the courtyard, where they hurried at the sound of his voice.

He shakes his head again. "No," he says. "Of course you have not been with him." He waves his fingers at their audience. "Inside, all of you. Leave us." Shuffling, whispering, moving with much less alacrity than when they raced outside, everyone returns to the studio.

"My dear." Antonia, who has hung back, watching from the covered walkway that runs along the courtyard, surprises them. She steps out of the shadows, takes her husband's arm. "Do you suppose that—"

"I suppose," Prospero interrupts his wife, whirling to face her, "that you should be inside. I suppose that you are interfering in things which are none of your affair."

"But I—"

The same wave, the same dismissive gesture he has just given to the servants. "I will not tell you twice."

After she is gone, Prospero closes his eyes, folds his arms. When he looks up again, he has decided something. "Wait here," he says, then turns and walks toward the workshop.

What did her mother want to say? What *could* she have said? Here, waiting with Paolo in the fading day, Vini fights the urge to run after Antonia, to chase down the little bit of light she has taken with her into the house. Instead she turns to the young man beside her, grateful, wanting to tell him so. But before she can say a word, her father is back.

"You," he snaps at Paolo, waving, always waving. "Inside, where you belong."

Vini hopes she will be strong. She hopes she will not crumple under the hurt of it, when he laughs at what she wants. When he pats her arm and tells her she has overreached. When he sends her into supper like the rest.

They are alone, and her father stares at her, intent, wordless. Then, after the briefest of agonies, he holds up the scroll of paper he has carried with him from the shop. He unrolls it in front of Vini. It is her drawing. The puppets, sun lapping at the edges of their fancy costumes, perform for the audience, who stand in the comfort of a huge church-shaped shadow.

"Here," he says, pointing to the page. "You have got the light wrong."

Vini looks at her father, then at the drawing. She nods.

"Next time," Prospero tell her, "you will know better."

She was not onstage in this dream, she was in the audience. She craned her neck, trying to see, as flute music floated out over the square. Two children in front of her shrieked with delight when the curtains drew back and the puppets appeared.

She recognized the princess's dress and her green slippers right away. But this time something new had been added to the story. Instead of the snarling dragon, there was a handsome knight beside the pretty little puppet. The young pair held hands and bowed, then began to dance. The knight, even with his glistening armor, moved effortlessly across the stage. Because she was watching from far away and could not see their strings, it looked as if he was really lifting the princess as they twirled together, sparkling and spinning like a jeweled top.

Drawn by the music and the dance, she pressed through the crowd, moving closer and closer to the stage. At last she reached the front row, only to hear a harsh, broken sound over the flute music. She wondered why no one else seemed to realize that the noise was coming from the puppets, that as they danced they were crying. From this close range, it was easy to see why. Each time a string was yanked and their bodies flew into the air, hurled this way and that, the puppets cried out. Each time the audience applauded and laughed, if you listened closely, you could hear them sob: "Stop, please stop! It hurts!"

Chapter Eleven

WHEN SOMETHING YOU HAVE HOPED AND PRAYED FOR FINALLY happens, it is seldom exactly as you dreamed. The first day Vini works in her father's studio, it is raining. And cold. Though she would love to wear her fur-lined robe, she knows better. She arrives in a plain woolen dress and accepts a leather apron like the ones the other students have fastened over their shirts and leggings.

For a moment, tying on the apron and standing just inside the door, Vini is swept by shyness. Some of the apprentices are talking by the window, one is sweeping, others are already seated at the benches along the common table. Where is her place? Will her father let her sit with the rest? She knows these young men, has spoken to many of them. But suddenly, they seem unapproachable, anointed.

"Good morning, Signorina." Paolo is not using his low, comic bow. Instead, he nods toward her and then indicates a seat at the table. "Will you join us?"

The studio falls silent as everyone looks in her direction. Then, like Moses parting the sea, a huge figure leaves the hearth and comes toward her from across the room. Prospero, so unsettled by Vini's artistic ambitions just a week ago, now seems convinced that today was his idea. He brushes past Paolo, as if the boy were not there and holds out his arm to his daughter. "Ah," he says, "I see our newest student has arrived." He escorts Vini in a long, parade-like march around the table to a place on the bench opposite Paolo's. Ignoring her struggle to fit her skirts over the bench and under the trestle, he takes up his own position, standing at the head of the table, his back to the window's damp light.

At this signal, the rest of the apprentices, yawning, full of Silvana's rolls and fig jam, seat themselves on both benches and wait. Surprisingly, Prospero does not mention Vini by name, although, of course, every man in the room knows who she is. Instead he launches into one of his lengthy speeches, this one about Caterina Vigri. With rhetorical flourishes and sweeping gestures, he tells them what they already know: how this "mere woman," this almost saint who lived in Bologna a hundred years ago, painted the Christ child with such tenderness and skill that He came to life in her arms one Christmas night.

"Who are we, then, to question where Our Lord distributes grace?" Prospero is pacing, the way he always does when he discourses. "And who are we to refuse to nurture a talent He has seen fit to plant?"

Prospero's change of heart leaves Vini tense and nervous. And something more. Is it pride she feels, uncurling like a green shoot, when he talks about Caterina but looks at her?

"Nor is Vigri the only woman who has distinguished herself as an artist." Prospero strikes his lion's pose, leaning across the table, meeting them with his fierce eyes. "Every man here has heard of Italy's bright new light, the noble Anguissola's daughter, Sofonisba. Her fame traveled to Spain, gentleman, and she has served that court as royal portraitist for over eight years now." He clears his throat, waits for nods and murmurs of approval. "The great Michelangelo himself took an interest in her youthful work. How many of you can hope for such an honor?"

Someone else's daughter has made good. A nobleman's child. The best families, it seems, encourage their females. And if Vini has always wanted to paint, her father has always yearned for aristocracy. Is this endless diatribe, then, this fancy argument, designed to persuade Prospero himself as well as his students? Has he finally decided, as a last resort, to pour his energies into shaping the career of his only child?

Vini knows that her mother has not yet told him about the baby. Mama does not want to risk disappointing Father with another lost child. But how long will she keep her news to herself? And will it be too late, once she announces it, for Prospero to call back all this passionate talk? Or will he, like a deft gardener jamming a rock into a tiny spring, deflect his plans from Vini then, pouring all his hopes and dreams into the future of his son?

"We live in a city that has long encouraged females to rise to examples set by men." Her father's great mane of hair has fallen across one eye, his voice has settled into a hypnotic purr. "Was it not at the University of Bologna that a woman lectured on law two hundred years ago?"

Vini has heard of the legendary Novella Calderini, how the beautiful woman had to stand behind a screen while she taught, so as not to distract her male pupils. Could her father possibly intend, after this grand speech, to separate Vini from the rest, to have her work by herself? She does not care, she decides, so long as she gets to draw and paint. Wherever she sits, she will smell the mineral spirits, the oil, the sweet, dusty scent of chalk.

"And do you suppose, gentlemen, that Caterina de' Medici is ruling France with her pretty face alone?" It is as though her father has discovered something new, something he can justify. This potential of women has a shape, a history he can point to. If he keeps talking, he is likely to take them all back to Greece, to the poetess Sappho, to the Amazons, to Athena. Vini's muscles are trembling, ready. She does not want to travel backward, she wants to move ahead. She wants to pick up the pencil waiting on the table in front of her. A new pencil. A new chance.

"Do not be misled, *garzoni*, by the sweet countenance you see among us today." For an instant, Vini feels all the students' eyes on her, a palpable rush of attention. Then they are watching Prospero again.

"My daughter will justify my faith in her." Who is this new father who turns toward her now? He is as proud and pompous as ever, but he looks at her when he speaks. And hard as it is to believe, he is speaking on her behalf.

"I have asked her to join our group, not as a dainty visitor but as an artist of promise." His gaze, his face, his voice—they travel across the room, they seek her out. She is filled with humility, with fear, with a violent hope. "Mark my words, *artiste,* her gift will redeem its frail vessel. If I have an eye, if I have a talent, they will bear fruit here."

He points now, his tapering finger like God's, indicating Vini. She is overwhelmed that in seven short days it has happened. Father is now committed to her, in the only way he can be. In the days and months and years ahead, she realizes, he will take credit for her work, her successes, her very life.

But if Prospero, at long last, is giving Vini an opportunity to prove herself, many in his *bottega* are not. Several of the apprentices, who have remained quiet while Prospero is in front of them, are merciless the minute he passes out the drawing boards and turns his back to arrange a still life. "God is watching," one of them on her left hisses while Father groups fruit and a bowl on a cloth-covered chest.

Her father has left a drawing board at her place. Vini will, for better or worse, be sitting with the rest of the class. "Your pride is an offense to nature," the boy on her right warns her. He pauses only a second when Prospero turns, resumes as soon as his back is to them once more. "Do not expect pity from any man here when this work breaks you."

Vini is stunned to see that this newest persecutor is the butcher's son, Ludovico Carracci, one of her father's favorites. He is a heavy fellow, slow and raw-boned—a good fit for his nickname, *Bue*, the Ox.

"Silence, *Bue*," someone commands. Her defender is across the table, but even without looking up, Vini knows Paolo's voice. Ludovico does, too.

"Some may have their own reasons for welcoming you here," he responds, looking at Vini but speaking to her champion. "As for me, I would rather paint beside a bitch in heat."

Vini has never talked to this young man at length, nor to any of the apprentices, with whom she has exchanged only a few words when they have wandered into the kitchen or been sent to the main house on errands for Prospero. But she knows one thing about this redheaded fellow whose eyes are always half closed and who moves as if he were walking under water: he draws like an angel. Over and over, from her vantage point outside the studio window, Vini has watched her father hold up his work for all the rest to study.

Paolo is out of his seat now, his hand on his waist, as if the knife he carried last week were still there. The look on his face, angry and set, promises more trouble. Trouble Vini must avoid.

She does not answer the Ox, only glances briefly, pleadingly at Paolo, then moves her paper and lapboard away from Ludovico, sliding down the bench to concentrate on her father's careful hands placing an artichoke and an orange just so, just so.

"Do you think you are wanted here?" the Ox persists, ignoring Paolo, who has crossed the room to stand behind him, and leaning across the distance Vini has put between them. His voice is a whispered snarl. "There is no place but Hell for a woman who wants to be a man."

Suddenly Vini wishes her father *had* chosen to separate her from the rest of his students. If only she could be curled in her bed right now, with Cesare at her feet! If only she could bring her drawings to Papa after the others have left.

"Please," she says, whether to Paolo or the Ox she is not sure. "I only want to try, I only want—"

"Signor Zappi!" The one voice that can end this confusion booms out across the room. "I hope you do not feel above the humble still life I have supplied for you?" Does Father know what has happened? Or is he simply outraged to find Paolo out of his seat?

Her mouth is dry, and a tiny sliver of pain has established itself between her eyes. But she cannot let Paolo take the blame for this disturbance. "It is my fault, Father." She stops, corrects herself. "*Maestro*. I asked Signor Zappi to help me sharpen my pencil."

Prospero frowns, waits until Paolo has walked back to his place.

"You should have asked me for help." Ludovico has timed his jab perfectly; Father is still watching Paolo. "I can give you what you need a lot better than that weasel."

Painting, Vini thinks, will be a great deal easier than holding her tongue. Her mother prayed to Saint Margaret and got a baby. But to whom can Vini turn for patience? She is afraid to call on Saint Luke, patron of artists. Saint or not, Luke was a man.

Mercifully, both she and her tormentor are forced to look at Prospero now. He holds up a wine goblet he has added to the still life. It is silver but has been carved like a diamond: each of its faceted sides reflects light. "An object eats up space, *garzoni*," Father tells them, ignoring the fact that he has called them all, even Vini, *boys*. "See how it attracts light and air." He raises the cup high, twirling it between his fingers. "See how it transforms the space around it."

And her Heavenly Father? He is a man, too. Vini wonders, not for the first time, if what she dreams of, what she aches for, is wrong. *I do not want to be a man.* She wishes she could scream it into Ludovico's small pink ear, curled like a slug on the side of his head. *I want to celebrate God's world! I want to touch His face!*

But it is not just this boy whose mind is closed, whose heart is set against her. The others are whispering, too. Laughing and nudging each other whenever Father turns away, whenever Vini coughs or moves her head or shifts in her seat. Here, in this place she has yearned after, has dreamed so long of finding herself, she is besieged.

By everyone except Paolo. Like the rest, he watches her every move, but Paolo's watching is different. It is a sort of devotion, as if he is memorizing her steps, as if he plans to draw each of her minutes, her whole day.

"I wish you to take note that even this cup has architectural proportions." Prospero lowers the goblet. "That where it stands, this simple vessel has a role in your picture."

He folds his arms, and Vini wonders if he remembers that, only minutes before, he called her a "vessel," too. She hopes he will not turn away, will not give the students time to whisper about *simple vessels*. "We may twist or stretch the human body to show tension, but there must always be still objects like this, building blocks of space.

"Here?" Prospero touches the side of the cup, trails his finger into the air behind it. "This is one of the sightlines that run out from the vanishing point. See how the scale increases as you advance toward the viewer?" He moves the cup toward several of the boys, then sets it down again.

And now he tells them to look, look, look. To study the goblet, the fruit, and the bowl until their eyes know every difference, every curve and line and hue that distinguishes this cup from other cups, this bowl from another, this orange from all the rest. Only then, he says, should they draw. Only then will they be ready to do what God does: create life on a blank page.

If the others are laughing now, Vini does not hear it. If her father stops and stands beside her while she works, she does not notice. She is focused on the tiny, intricate realities of the crack in the wooden bowl, the light on the cup, the fuzzy blush of the grapes. She is tracing the whorled maze of the artichoke's sharp leaves. She is traveling across the dimpled, vaguely lit surface of the orange. *Abbondanza. Plenty,* she thinks. *The world is full of blessings, if only you know how to look.*

It is hard to say how much time has passed; she is immune to hunger or fatigue. She is hardly human, she has penetrated so deeply into fruit and wood and sparkling silver. She is a partner to each, a loving consciousness that holds, cherishes. Perhaps that is how God feels about her? Perhaps, and the thought astonishes her, He loves her as much as she loves Him?

When she is almost finished, still dizzy from the fullness inside her, something tears her from the drawing. She looks up to see the Ox and a boy called Salvatore staring at her work. Her hand stops and she holds her breath. Instinctively, Vini looks across the table to Paolo. But he is hard at work.

Salvatore is clearly perplexed by what Vini has drawn. The younger boy's brows are knitted, and his full, cherub's lips part to reveal a bad tooth. But it is not his earnest consternation that disturbs Vini, like a flea crawling across her shoulders—it is Ludovico. If the expression the Ox wears when he looks at Vini herself is unsettling, the face he turns now on her drawing is astounding in its fury. "You have betrayed your sex," he growls, glaring not at Vini, but at her still life. It is as if the page has insulted him, as if he wants to take it in his hands and tear it apart.

He elbows the other boy, whispers behind his hand. "I pity this one's husband, eh? I will warrant there is a prick under that skirt." Though his voice is loud enough for Vini to hear, he does not watch her, stares only at the drawing. His cheeks are ruddy but his knuckles are white. How badly he must want to grab the sketch from her!

Vini glances across the table at Paolo, who clearly has not heard them. He is still bent over his own drawing board, forming slow and careful lines. He looks up frequently to check the fruit and the bowl, as if they might have moved since his last stroke. But when he finds Vini's eyes on him, he abandons the orange and grapes, trusting them to stay where they are. He smiles at her.

Something in that smile makes Vini remember how new and strong she felt as she worked, how proud she is of her drawing. She longs to show it to him, to hold it up for his certain approval. She settles, instead, for smiling back.

It is a mistake. The two boys beside her snicker and point. "Paolo has a new teacher, it seems." Ludovico's face is twisted into a simpering mask, his mouth pursed, his eyes opened nearly to normal size. "He watches you, Signorina Fontana, more than our Master."

Vini turns back to her drawing. "What lessons is he learning from you, pray tell?" Salvatore has joined in now, jabbing deeper in an effort to please his friend. "Do you give private classes, or can anyone attend?"

Paolo has returned to his drawing, and the bullies have kept their voices too low for the others to hear. Vini feels the tears start, manages to keep them at bay. But she is close to risking a scene, to provoking her father's wrath. She is ready to tell these students that the lessons they are most in need of involve courtesy and good manners. Before she can, Prospero appears behind the Ox. He places one hand on the young man's shoulder, the other gestures toward his drawing of the goblet. "Your drawing lacks perspective," he scolds. "This is a fine study of a cup, *if* it were under your nose." He pats Ludovico's bulky arm. "But it is not beneath that prominent feature, is it?"

The Ox lowers his head, shamed, but does not answer. Vini's father repeats his question. "Is it, Sir?"

Ludovico shakes his head at last, and Prospero moves on to stand behind his daughter. Vini stiffens, anticipating her father's ringed hand on her back, but he does not touch her. Worse, he does not speak. For the length of half a Miserene, he stands in silence. At last he coughs. *"Sì,"* he says. Yes. That is all. Finally, *"Justo."* Right. Then he is gone.

When Vini planned today, of course, it happened very differently. She imagined her father and she would be face-to-face, like Blessed Mary and the Angel of the Annunciation. Prospero would walk toward her, offering his words like a lily. She would study his face, see the devotion in his dark eyes, a candle in a cave. "I have waited all my life," her dream father would tell her, "to find someone who paints like you."

Sì. And then, *Justo.* Two words. Vini has been blessed, she acknowledges, with one more word than her mother won from Prospero years before. *Buono,* he told Antonia then. Good. It had been enough. And though she has dreamed it differently, it is enough for Vini, too. It is enough, after all, that her work is good.

The hard looks, Ludovico's rudeness, the others' laughter—they mean nothing now. Vini has been lifted up by two small words. She has been given protection from the discouragement of rain and cold feet, from her mother's sadness, and from the loneliness of women who weave gossip and tapestries behind closed doors. She has been saved from endless hours of talking to Ginevra and Zia about wedding trunks and tailors, about keeping breasts firm and skin soft, about garden parties and musicales and who has the finest gowns and who the worst.

Her father wanted to hold her drawing up. Vini knows this, as well as she knows the orange and the artichoke and the grapes she has just sketched. In the pause before he spoke, she sensed his eagerness, the approval he kept in check. He wanted to use

Chapter Twelve

BY THE TIME PROSPERO DISMISSES THEM, VINI IS EXHAUSTED, not only from hugging her board hour after hour, but from the strain of trying to block out the whispers, the laughter meant to frighten and discourage her.

Making sure she is not the first to leave, she stands, tightening the damp knot of hair at the back of her neck for what seems like the hundredth time today. She walks slowly toward the door, which is, of course, not fast enough.

Salvatore, with a broad smile that Vini can read as neither disdain nor friendship, scrambles to walk beside her. He waves a bony finger in her face. "You do nice work," he says, as though she had asked for his opinion. "For a female."

Now the Ox joins them, smirking, and Vini realizes it is all a joke. But still she turns to Salvatore, ignoring his friend. *"Grazie,"* she tells him, forcing her knees into a modest curtsy. "God works miracles"—she barely smiles, lowers her eyes—"even through fragile instruments." Without raising her eyes, she brushes past them and leaves the shop, taking care to hold her skirts above the paint-spattered floor.

"*Il Maestro* wanted to use your drawing as a model," Paolo tells her when she reaches the fountain in the courtyard. The two of them meet as if they had planned it, neither surprised by the other being there. Even though it is still drizzling. Even though the iron-colored sky is heavy, threatening.

"Yes," Vini says. "But it is too soon."

"Do not worry about the others, Little One." Paolo searches her face, reaches for her hand. "They will all come to admire you as I do."

"Paolo." She does not know how to say it. "It would help if *you* admired me a little *less*." She wishes she had said nothing. Another day of teasing might be easier than seeing that sad, lost look of his.

"It is just that the others notice," she adds. "They think we are . . ." This time, without artifice, she lowers her gaze. "They whisper." She does not intend to sigh or to let her voice tremble, but she does both. "They speak ill of us."

"You are right." Paolo scans the courtyard behind them. There are no stragglers from the studio, but even so, when he turns back to Vini, he lets go her hand. "I want to kiss your fingers, but I will not," he says. "I want to brush that raindrop from your chin."

Vini nods, smiles, then wipes it away herself. "I wanted to show you my drawing this morning. I wanted to sit beside you at the table."

He says nothing in response, but his smile is open, laced with relief, as if the sun has suddenly broken through the low, sullen clouds above them. But then Silvana's eldest daughter comes hurrying from the main house. Vini turns in time to catch the worried look on the woman's face.

"*Scusi, Padrona.*" Betta has known Vini since she was a teenager and Vini was a child, yet she has never called Vini anything but Mistress. "It is your mother. She is ill."

Vini remembers her mother's secret. Remembers the graveless, nameless babies who were never born. She glances at Paolo, and now it is she who wants to hold his hand.

"*Per favore.* Come quickly." Already Betta is racing back across the courtyard. She does not look behind her, assumes her mistress is following.

"Ciao, Paolo," Vini says, though there is so much more she had meant to tell him. And then she is running, her skirts lifted, thin jets of rain spraying her ankles, to catch up with Betta.

When she reaches her mother's apartment, Vini stops just outside the open door. There is no one in the sewing room, but she can hear noises coming from the bedroom. "Mama?"

There is no answer, only a moan that pulls Vini into the room.

When she pushes aside the heavy curtains around her mother's bed, she finds Antonia curled like a child in the center of the mattress. She is holding her knees, rocking and whimpering. It is a low animal sound she makes, a soft complaint Vini has never heard from her before. "Mama?"

Antonia raises her head from the pillows, looks at Vini through a veil of pain. Her hair is damp, uncombed, and for an instant there is only distance, only confusion in her eyes. But then she knows her visitor. "Vini," she says. Just that, before she grabs tighter hold of her knees and calls on someone else: "Santa Margareta, spare me."

Vini is uncertain how to help. She lowers herself gently onto the sheets, sits by her mother's feet. Which is when she smells the unmistakable odor of vomit, sees the bowl on the table beside the bed. "Ai," Antonia groans. "Ai, Blessed Mother."

Betta does not knock, says nothing as she bustles into the room and changes the filled bowl for another. Again Vini's mother raises her head, again struggles to make sense of what she sees. "*Grazie*," she says, still curled, still slick with sweat.

"My mother is making a broth," Betta announces. "It will stop the sickness."

"No." Antonia rallies yet. "Tell Silvana no." She uncurls to insist, to shake her head, and then falls back against the pillows. "I cannot eat."

"Mama, what is wrong?"

"Nothing is wrong, Padrona," Betta answers for her mistress. "It is the way of the world, that is all." She wipes Antonia's forehead with a cloth. "Some babies make you sick in the morning, some make you sick at night." She turns the cloth over, presses it again to Antonia's brow. "Your mother's baby is making her sick in the afternoon."

After a few minutes, though, Antonia seems improved. Betta helps her sit up before she leaves, and now she asks Vini to tell her everything. How was the class? How did Prospero like Vini's work? Her eyes have blue shadows under them, like crushed violets, but she is animated, eager.

Vini tells about Father's speech, about frail vessels and carelessly sewn talent, and Antonia nods. "He likes my work, Mama. I think he has decided that a daughter who paints is better than . . ." She stops, looks at her mother, then looks away. "Than nothing," she says.

Vini does not tell her fear, how once a son is born, she is not at all sure Papa will care about a talented daughter. But Antonia hears the words Vini has spoken only in her heart. "Your father does not need to know about the baby until later." She leans back, smiles. "For now it is our secret, yes?"

Gratitude swamps Vini. And a guilty relief. More days, more months. A gift of silence. "Thank you, Mama."

"I almost told him that day in the courtyard." Antonia is whispering, delighted to play the role of conspirator. "When he called Paolo from the studio, when he accused you of . . ."—she touches the carnelian beads, the persimmon-colored jewels at her throat— ". . . of something you did not do."

Yes. Vini knows it now. Her mother would have told Father about the baby. If she had not been banished before she could speak, she would have put her happy news between Vini and his anger. She takes Antonia's hands, presses the white fingers in her own. "Mama, you should have seen what we did today." She tells about the cup, how everyone in the room knew it better than a dear friend's face, better than the way to church.

She is still talking when Betta comes back, places a bowl of steaming soup beside them. "Make her eat, Signorina," she instructs Vini. "It will seal the baby inside."

But when she is gone again, Vini despairs of following orders. Her mother takes one look at the rich mist peeling off the bowl and turns away. She groans as if the sickness is starting again, closes her eyes. "He liked your drawing, eh?"

"*Sì,*" Vini tells her. "But some did not." She describes the way Ludovico hounded her, the way the others laughed and pointed.

"You are a rose whispering in the wind, not everyone will hear you." Antonia opens her eyes and focuses on her daughter. "It is a blessing and a curse, this gift of yours."

The two look at each other, and in that moment Vini sees the architecture of her mother's face. Like the cup she sketched this morning, its contours are a thing of wonder, newly discovered— every turn, every plane swept toward beauty.

And then the nausea comes again. Antonia pulls into herself, heaving. Vini holds her mother's hair, just as her mother held hers when Vini was little and had the croup. Antonia bolts against her and, as the sickness grows, makes empty wretching sounds above the bowl. But she produces nothing, and lies back, spent.

"When your brother is born," she says, and the words feel sharp as the shards of vase Vini sent skittering across the courtyard at summer's end. "When your brother is born, things will be different." Antonia is not looking at Vini anymore but staring into the air, at something Vini cannot see. "There is more than one way to prove yourself, my love. You can help me take care of your brother, too." She reaches for Vini's hand, covers it with her feverish fingers. "You and I together? We will make your father so happy."

This vision of her mother's, this brother-savior, rises between them, and Vini understands she cannot share how she feels with Antonia. Still, for a moment, she tries.

"Mama, once the baby is born, Papa will not think of anything else. I like working in the studio." *Like. What a feeble word!* Antonia does not know about her trips to the shed, the stolen paper, the drawings. "I need to be there."

"You will see, love," Antonia tells her, hardly listening, smiling into the future. "Everything will be better."

Mama, Vini wants to say. *Mama, the baby will have pink feet and curled toes. It will not walk on water. When it opens its mouth, it will cry and fuss and drool. It will not speak in tongues.*

But Vini does not say any of this. Instead she waits, silent, at the foot of the bed, until the gentle, even breathing, the small rise and fall of Antonia's shoulders, tell her that her mother is asleep. *There is a painting I want to do, Mama. It is of you and me in your little garden. I will paint the two of us, laughing and sweating under the sun, or running out to dig after the rain, when the ground is soft and smells like clover.*

Vini hears Silvana in the kitchen, and when she walks into the close, luscious-smelling room, the old woman is scolding her daughter. "Not hot," she tells Betta. "It is supposed to be warm, like for a baby, no? How many times did I say it, how many times?"

"Hot soup," Betta tells her mother, shrugging, "will turn warm." She gathers up the laundry and walks to the door. "Right, Signorina?" she asks, passing Vini; then, without waiting for an answer, she is gone. Betta could have filled a tub here, but Vini knows she prefers to do the wash with the other maids at the fountain in town. She has seen them, in a laughing cluster, a knot of rough goodwill and loud, off-color jokes.

"That one is always in a hurry," Silvana says to nobody in particular. She pulls a chair out for Vini but does not stop pounding batter against the sides of the large wooden bowl she holds. "Never listens, never did."

Vini sticks a finger into the bowl and gets a rap on the knuckles from Silvana's spoon. But not before she has tasted the sweet, thick paste. She rolls it around in her mouth, smiling, then whistles to the heap of fur in the corner by the hearth. Cesare opens his eyes and lifts his snout. He sniffs the air and blinks, then yawns and ambles toward her to be lifted up.

"Mama is sleeping," Vini tells Silvana. She pulls the little dog onto her lap and scratches the tender hollows behind his ears. "But she would not take any of the soup."

"Good." Silvana stops beating and puts down the bowl. She twists some leaves from one of the herb bundles above the hearth, then crumbles them into a mortar. She talks as she grinds. "You must add this to the cooled soup. A few leaves every day. It will give Signora strength."

"Silvana," Vini looks over Cesare's tiny head, "will Mama be all right?"

"She will be better by spring, Preziosa." Silvana must be telling the truth, Vini decides; her pestle is making steady, reassuring thumps against the mortar. "Long before her birthing time, the sickness will stop."

"And the baby?" Vini watches the old woman closely, sees the way her hands suddenly slow, then stop. She remembers the other waiting times, the times that led to nothing but her father's crusting over, turning away, hardening his heart.

"The baby?" Silvana is grinding again, but faster, wilder. "I cannot say."

"Will it live this time?" Vini remembers her mother's bright, urgent eyes.

"God knows this, Preziosa. You must ask Him." Silvana puts the mortar aside and wipes her hands on her apron. "Tell me about the class now. Did you show those upstarts a thing or two?"

The elderly servant takes a seat across from her, and suddenly Vini is telling her everything, everything she did not tell Antonia: how the whispers of the others tunneled into her heart, how the teasing made her wish she could work alone with her father. How she curtsied to Carracci. And how it seems even her mother thinks roses are too soft to be heard.

When she is finally out of words, the old woman laughs. She shakes a long finger in Vini's face. "You are no rose, Preziosa. You are a wind out of the south. There will be no stopping you.

"And Signor Carracci? He is a sly, sneaking marten. A weasel that should be skinned and used to fend off fleas."

"But . . ."

"But what, Signorina Fontana?" Silvana is smiling her toothless, infant's smile. "He can snarl and snap all he wants, that one." She leans forward, a wrinkled Sybil. "You will do what you will do.

"And what you will do now," she adds, leaving her seat to stand by the door, "is have supper with the Signore. He is already at table."

Vini is glad she has an excuse for being late. Her father's plate is nearly empty. "Mama is not feeling well enough to come down," she says as soon as she is seated opposite him.

Prospero inclines his head, the barest of nods, then sips his wine. "Your mother's constitution is frail," he says, his voice neutral, as if he were describing a horse or a dog. "What challenges some, defeats others. I daresay this pigeon would have defeated her utterly." He glances briefly at the dish in front of him, then studies Vini.

"You did well today. You vindicated my faith in you."

The tiny bird on her plate is curled, its headless torso hunched under its wings. "Thank you, Father." She pushes the meat with her fork but does not eat.

"Your bloodline is clear; you are a Fontana, not an ink-smudged Bonardis. We will show the world that a daughter of Fontana is the equal of others' sons.

"But you must stop those foolish lessons with the old priest." Her father puts down his glass, holds her eyes. "My friend Signor Aldrovandi—the tall gentleman you met at the banquet this summer? He is a professor of natural science, remember?"

Vini nods.

"I am doing paintings for his new text. In return, Ulisse has agreed to work with you on nature sketches."

"*Sì,* Papa." Vini is thrilled at the prospect of learning about trees, the way their barks look, how their seedpods ride the air like thistle down.

She moves the braised fennel from one side of her plate to the other, but still she does not eat. Her father has torn her in half, as usual. Half of her is furious at him for the way he speaks of Mama. The other half is filled with pride at his praise.

And then, as if he knows exactly what happened in the studio, Prospero changes topics. "You will have to deal with jealousy, Lavinia. And small minds."

She raises her head, looks at him. "Ludovico . . ."

"He is a fine painter, that one."

"But he—"

"A fine painter and a poor sport." He sips more wine. "So long as you know large truths, Lavinia, small minds cannot harm you. Rest in your birthright, Daughter. And in the knowledge that your father saw the spark of talent others would deny."

For a moment, Vini can almost believe that this was Prospero's idea from the start. He is her redeemer now, the Columbus who has stumbled on her wild, untamed gifts, who will nurture them and, like the greatest teachers, find depths that will astonish even

Vini herself. It is as if she never snuck or plotted or pushed Paolo into lie after lie.

"So you are not angry with Signor Zappi?" She asks it as lightly, as carelessly as she can. "You do not blame him for my deception?"

"Your deception?" Again the nod, the almost imperceptible inclination of that great, dark head.

"For representing my work as his own." She cannot succeed at the cost of her dear friend's downfall. He has protected her, believed in her, and he must not lose his place in the studio. "It was not Paolo's idea."

Her father tosses his napkin on the table, pushes his chair back. "That buffoon does not have the brains for subterfuge, Daughter. Mediocrity has no imagination."

He has said the same thing about Mama, has dismissed her with the same wave of his hand. "Then you will not punish him?"

"He deserves no punishment, Lavinia, just as he deserves no praise."

Is this love? The way Prospero confides his disdain, the way he looks at her as if he is looking into a mirror?

"On the contrary, it is I who am to be censured."

"You, Father?"

"My blood brought you talent, but I did not see it right away. I did not consider that a great gift will take root wherever it is planted."

The pigeon's breast is red with sauce; it is piled with hazelnuts and raisins. *What to you see when you look at me, Papa?*

"We have lost time, you and I." He counts on his long, pale fingers. "Three, maybe four years. You see the price Zappi's parents paid by letting him choose one career, then another." He smiles, but it is an ironic, sad smile. "Not that the boy had any talent to begin with."

Vini waits.

"We must move quickly if you are to assist me with background painting next year."

Assist? She is still angry with Papa for speaking ill of Paolo, but her faithless heart leaps like a bird in her chest. She cannot help seeing already the way the plaster on the mural walls will look, the way the charcoal sketches will wait, like wishes or prayers, to be filled with color and life.

"And in a few years more, you will be working on figures, and then on portraits. The Farnese family are fond of you, and you will meet the Medici when you come with me to Florence. Everyone will want work from you."

Florence! Vini imagines herself in the homes of these fine families, in their great halls, their showy bedrooms. "Wonderful, Signora," she will tell her noble sitters, "the way your hand rests on that Bible. You have a natural grace, Heaven knows. This will not take long." Arranging a vase, opening a window so the light streams in and falls on the face just so.

"Yes." Prospero's voice does not rise, his hands do not move, and his eyes are empty of light. But this stillness is what Vini knows of him, what she recognizes as his pleasure. "My name will go on, the studio will continue. All because we acted in time."

The pigeon, the honeyed squash, the lentil cake. She cannot eat a single bite. She is too excited, too angry, too full of the feelings he always stirs in her: pain and pride and doubt. *Do you see yourself in my eyes, Papa? or do you see me?*

Chapter Thirteen

STUDYING WITH ULISSE ALDROVANDI HAS TWO ADVANTAGES. First, the naturalist Prospero has chosen to work with his daughter is a kind man who finds friends everywhere. Not much older than Father, Ulisse is slender bordering on emaciated, but his voice and laugh sound as if they come from someone three times his size. Vini wonders why he does not scare away the birds they find in the park. "There you are," he greets each one heartily from below their perches in the cypress and the hemlock. "Give us some of your time, good Signora" (or "Signore" if the markings are bright). "You are too splendid to forget."

The second and even more delightful aspect of being Ulisse's pupil, is that Vini's classroom is outdoors. Though she must wear the veil of an unmarried woman when they set out for their lessons, she always throws it back when they reach the park off Strada Maggiore. She prowls the woods and hikes along streams, bringing back pods and thistles, salamanders and moss. "An excellent specimen," Ulisse tells her, turning each one over and over between his skinny fingers. "See here, where the spore will escape? And here, where the side that gets no sun has turned white?"

And then they set to work, the two of them. Ulisse saves the things he will take back to his study, drying leaves and seeds and butterfly wings in a special wooden press he has devised; Vini sketches with charcoal or ink. For luscious hours, they sprawl on grassy slopes or in the shade of manicured public gardens, working at what her mentor calls "field study," though Vini thinks she has never had more fun in all her life. To be free of the street veil, to be under the sky without having to sneak or lie, to tramp for miles without anyone telling her where to go or what to do—surely, this is how men and angels must feel!

Once, after Vini has grown easy with her tutor, she begs to take Cesare with them. The dog is hysterical with happiness as he yips at their heels, flushes birds from hedges, and generally ruins their day. "I am so sorry, Signor Aldrovandi," Vini hears herself saying again and again. "I should not have brought him."

"On the contrary, Signorina Fontana," Ulisse finally tells her, endearing himself to her forever. "This tiny beast may have upset *our* plans, but it is perfectly in tune with Nature's." He settles himself beside her, pulling out a pen and the small leatherbound book he keeps in his vest. "I had best take notes for my volume on predators."

Vini, who cannot tell whether her teacher is joking, watches

Cesare scramble after an errant goose, then retreat as the large bird tires of the game and comes after him, wings spread, honking loudly. When she turns back to Aldrovandi, she notices that he is smiling broadly and has not written a single word in his book.

But the days have gotten colder, the birds are fewer, and the seeds are drying and blowing away. There will not be many more open-air lessons until the spring. Instead, Vini knows, she and Aldrovandi will be forced to sit by the fire in Papa's library, to pore over skeletons and dried leaves, the dusty remains of this precious autumn. Mad to keep the adventure going, eager to share it, Vini takes a carefully calculated risk after Prospero has set out on yet another trip to Florence.

"Signore," she asks her tutor one morning in late November, "do you suppose another student of Father's could accompany us today?" She busies herself, packing the knapsack Aldrovandi has given her, stacking the paper and bundling her pens and charcoal inside. "Signor Zappi has expressed to me his interest in the study of nature." (In fact, what Paolo said was, "I dream of the two of us taking walks where no one can see me hold you, where you and I can be alone.")

"Of course," Aldrovandi replies, so innocent that Vini immediately feels a twinge of guilt, "let us take him along. He can help with the bags. And perhaps he would not mind staying with you while I do some climbing and wading?"

Paolo does not mind at all. The three of them set out with a sack of fruit and cheese and six of Silvana's morning rolls. All afternoon they walk and sketch and, wrapped in woolen cloaks, soak up the fading warmth of the distant sun. When at last Ulisse hears a harsh call he insists is a rare species of dove, he begs their indulgence to follow it "just over the next hill."

In his absence, Paolo stops sketching and watches Vini work instead. It is as if he would rather do this than make anything himself, as if this is what he does best of all. She feels his eyes on her and smiles up at him, holding her paper out. "Do you like it?" she asks, knowing the answer.

"I like it very much, Signorina," he says. Then he leans to kiss her cheek. Vini looks after her tutor, whose rangy steps have taken him nearly out of sight, and does what she has yearned to do ever since spring: she touches the curls that frame her friend's face, the ringlets just above his forehead and on the back of his neck. A rush like water fills her ears, and now he is kissing her on the mouth. She wonders whose body this is, turning into air and light, rising for joy.

I am white, she thinks as he kisses her again, then finds her throat and presses his lips there, too. *I am a color you cannot mix.*

"Little One," Paolo says, or rather sighs, then pulls himself away to lie stretched full-length beside her on the faded grass. At first he brings her hand to his mouth, but then he holds it instead against his heart. "It hurts to love you so much."

I am the color of the dress I wore at confirmation.

"One day," he tells her, "you will be my wife. It must happen, or I will die."

When Aldrovandi returns, Vini and Paolo are sitting, perhaps only a little too close, sketching and chewing on the last of the tiny, hard apples they have found in the bottom of Silvana's sack. "Look! Look!" Vini's tutor calls to them, excited and flushed. "Look what I have!" Panting, he folds his long body beside them, emptying three pearl gray feathers onto the grass.

The days shorten and grow colder still. Paolo goes to visit his family in Imola, Advent passes, and Mama is feeling better. By the Vigil of the Nativity, on Christmas Eve, she is well enough to attend church. Ulisse, who has been working with Vini indoors and who feels like one of their family now, tags along. And because some guests Papa brought back from Florence have lingered, they, too, come to services.

Church is only a short way from the house, so everyone walks, leaving the carriage and horses at home. Aunt Beatrice is the one who proposed they "take the air," but Vini suspects it is only to show off her new cape and hat. Zia moves with a measured grace, a studied slowness that suggests she wants to make sure all of Bologna sees her new clothes.

The nave of Santissima Trinità is filled with flowers, white primroses and scarlet poppies. The sweet, heavy scent of their drooping heads blends with the incense, the beeswax tapers, and the perfume of the parishioners. Behind the bishop's throne, a lightless window set with colored glass waits for tomorrow's sun.

The Fontanas' pew is not at the front of the church, but it is near enough. Near enough for Vini to stop, at least for a minute, wishing that Paolo were with them, to be distracted by the silks, the furs, the tassels, capes, and jewelry. Everyone has worn their best to High Mass; they settle like swifts, chattering and noisy, while the procession makes its way down the central aisle. But then, when the organ wakes like a sobbing giant, filling the huge hall, the talk and laughter die away.

As the bishop reaches the altar and the priest and the others take their places below him, the great organ stops. In the crumb of quiet that follows, Vini holds her breath. Then, as the chorus sings the opening of the Mass, she feels what must be God's love, a sort of panic and splendor that fill her, that settle in her chest like wings, opening and closing as the music swells: *Kyrie eleison.* Lord, have mercy. *Christe eleison.* Christ, have mercy. *Kyrie eleison.* Lord, have mercy.

Tomorrow is the birthday of Our Savior. A man-child who will grow to hold the world in his hands. A blessed babe who will make kings tremble, who will bring us all to our knees. He will be mightier than nations, higher than this cathedral. *Domine Deus, Agnus Dei.* Lord God, Lamb of God. The voices fill the church, flinging themselves against the vaulted ceiling. *Filius Patris qui tollis peccata mundi . . .* Son of the Father who takes away the sins of the world . . .

How can Vini feel holy and lust-filled at once? She is missing

Paolo again, remembering the sound of his voice, the line of his legs stretched alongside hers on the grass. She searches the others' faces, wonders what images fill their heads. Beside her, Antonia wears a tiny smile, a sweet shadow of joy. Vini knows why, but no one else does. Not yet.

Why can't she be as happy as her mother? How can she celebrate one baby's birth and not another's? She studies Antonia, who has thrown off her fur cloak and is kneeling on one of the pillows they have brought with them. She appears no different, only a little thinner since the sickness. But inside her the seed is growing. Without light, in secret, Vini's brother is forming himself. *Lamb of God, grant us peace.* As everyone around her bows their heads, Vini cannot close her eyes without seeing him. The babe who waits to be born, the babe who has given her mother a Madonna's smile.

When she takes communion, she hardly dares look at the priest or the bishop. Even though they are just men like any others, she is afraid that in their robes they may be able to read her heart. Do they know how often she thinks of Paolo? Do they know how much she wishes he were beside her instead of with his own family? Do they know what she has just been thinking about the baby?

Father Anselmo and the bishop have been to her house, have sat and talked with Father, have drunk wine without blessing it first. But in their brocade chasubles, so heavy that two altar boys are needed to lift each of them when the great men move, they do not seem human. Holiness cloaks their gestures, their every step.

Once, when Father Anselmo was giving daily Mass, Vini noticed a splash of mud on his stole. But this is Christmas Mass and there is no stain, no blemish, except on her own soul.

On the walk home, Prospero is nearly jovial, joking with his guests about the end of Advent, which he confides will change his menu very little. Other more pious churchgoers break a long holy fast this time of year, but not Papa.

"When I was young, I watched two of my dearest companions die with Spanish bullets in their chests," he tells Ulisse and the rest. "Three years ago, an apprentice in my shop died of typhus." He stops in the street, places a hand on one of his guest's shoulders. "Fasting is fine for angels, my friends. But not for a man who knows each meal may be his last."

Vini studies her father from under her veil. *Dearest companions.* She tries to imagine Papa young, as young as that student in the *bottega* who died when she was twelve. He had been a strong, sinewy fellow, but the fever finished him in six days. She pictures a young man like that, laughing, playing at mock jousts or scrambling after a ball. *How did he feel, that younger, passionate Papa, when he went off to war with his friends and came back alone?*

Walking on each side of her, Mama and Zia Beatrice are talking about what has occupied them all day—the latest project the women of the church, the Sorority of Santissima, have undertaken for the congregation. They are making confirmation veils for the children of the poor, frothy white squares to place on the heads of new daughters of Christ.

Prospero has already made it plain how he feels about this latest effort of the Sorority. "Put a group of women together," he told his Florentines at the noon meal today, "and you are bound to hatch foolishness. Veils for the poor, eh?" He had picked his teeth, reached for more wine, and turned to Antonia. "Why not dance slippers for the lame, my dear? Or perhaps books for the blind?"

So now, while Papa is making light of fasting, Zia is loudly proclaiming far nobler aims. "Imagine," she says, clasping Mama's wrist, her veil thrown back, her eyes lit with zeal. "Imagine if we stitch a white rose in each corner. A rose and perhaps a lamb on the back."

"Goodness, 'Trice," Antonia says. "A lamb? Do you think we are all artists with a needle like you?"

"A cross, then." Zia releases Mama's arm and strides faster now, walking toward her vision. "Hundreds of little paupers coming to Christ in our gifts. Oh, Sister, won't it be perfect? A perfect act of charity?"

As if lured by her words, three figures step forward from under a colonnade that runs along the piazza. They are beggars, the one in the middle blind, helped by the other two, who hold him under his arms. They are wrapped against the cold with blankets and dirty, torn cloaks. Shoeless, they have bound rags around their

ankles and feet. The oldest—though, indeed, they are all old—
bows to Zia. Father and the men, who have been following behind,
nearly stumble into her when she stops short and pulls her fur cape
tight around her face.

"Signora, Signora," the old man says. *"Misericordia."* He holds
out his hand to Vini's aunt first, then to Vini and her mother.
"Mercy," he repeats. "Good Christmas to you all. Have mercy."

"Filthy!" Zia grabs Vini and pulls her away. "Don't let them get
near you, dear. They are covered with lice."

Now the blind beggar in the middle holds out his hand to
them, too. His skin is leathery and crossed with years and years
of wrinkles. His eyes appear to have been sewn shut; looking back
as her aunt pulls her ahead, Vini can see drops glistening in their
corners.

"Misericordia," the blind man echoes.

Prospero tries to pass by him, too, but the beggar grabs his
cloak. "Mercy, Signore."

Vini's father stands rigid for an instant, then brushes the blind
man's hand away. "Lying on Christmas, Sir?" he says. "You see as
well as I do, I warrant."

Ulisse, towering above them, surprises everyone except Vini.
"Greetings, Signori," he tells the beggars, using the same tone with
which he addresses birds and centipedes and bad dogs who chew
his field notes. "Let us pass, and there will be coins for you all."

Antonia falls back, touches her husband's arm. "It is the eve of

Our Lord's birth," she says, just loud enough for the visitors from Florence to hear. "There is no need to hide your generosity, my dear."

Vini's father looks at her darkly, then sighs and reaches into the purse on his belt. He and Ulisse throw coins onto the street and the three beggars rush to pick them up. "Ha!" Papa laughs, watching them scramble. "The blind one has found his first." He shakes his head. "He must have eyes in his fingers, no?"

He takes Antonia's arm now and hurries her ahead, the visitors flanking them. When they catch up with Vini and her aunt, the group divides again, the women in front, the men behind.

"You should not waste your husband's money on those street rats," Zia whispers too loudly. "Your job is to tighten his purse strings, not open them."

"'Trice," Antonia says, falling into step beside her sister, "do not scold so, you will get frown lines." She takes Zia's arm again. "Now tell me once more about those pauper children in our veils. What a lovely picture they will make!" She glances quickly at Vini, and there is the merest trace of a smile on her face before she turns back. It is not, Vini is relieved to observe, a Madonna's smile. It is sweet, but it is decidedly naughty.

Chapter Fourteen

WHEN FATHER'S GUESTS LEAVE FOR FLORENCE, HE GOES BACK TO work. Which means Vini does, too. She barely notices how cold it has gotten or how the days tumble past each other like hungry sheep. She is working on an altarpiece. Her trees, the ones she has spent hours sketching with Ulisse, will be used in the background of the center panel!

After Prospero has sketched the figures of Saint Catherine and the Holy Family, before Ludovico colors their hands and feet, Vini uses a carbon stick to draw woods and a stream tumbling down a hill behind them. Then she lays in the trees, the flowers, and two birds soaring in the sky overhead.

First she sketches and then she paints. She uses the drawings she has done in the park to choose the shapes of the leaves, the way the birds' wings arch, even the silhouettes of the grasses waving at the water's edge. As she works, she forgets everything around her. Forgets so completely that sometimes she wakes, as if from sleep, to find her father standing behind her. *"Buono,"* he may say. Or sometimes, *"Justo."* Nothing more.

The others, however, have plenty to say. Paolo is full of praise. "You have learned so much from Signor Aldrovandi, Little One." Their moments by the fountain or in the drafty shed are fewer and fewer, yet her friend seems genuinely glad for her. Glad, with only a touch of sadness. "You have left us all behind," he says. "There is no catching up to you, is there?"

Ludovico, of course, feels differently. "Backgrounds are nothing," the big fellow growls one morning, standing in a silly imitation of her father's pose, looking over Vini's shoulder as she works. "They are only the beginning for a real painter." He checks across the room to make sure Prospero is busy with another student. "But they are just the place for females."

Vini would like to defend herself. She pictures Bradamante, her fierce puppet heroine, imagines a flash of armor, the feel of a scabbard at her side. But here, among palettes and paints, she must fight a different battle. And so she takes a cue from her mother's hint of a smile.

Instead of a retort, she gives the Ox a dainty blush; she curtsies and compliments him on Saint Catherine's pink, plump hands. "The work of a serious painter," she tells him. She can say no more without tipping the balance between her desire to learn from this braggart and her shameful urge to hurt him as he has hurt her.

And then she uses her brush like a sword. She works them all into the ground. She paints better, faster, richer than any of the apprentices. And Prospero notices. One day he brings the distinguished scholar Carlo Sigonio to the studio. The two of them circle the room, stopping at all the drawing tables, coming finally to the altarpiece. "You see the pains we take," Father tells his famous guest, pointing to the center panel. "Even the leaves on these trees are accurate representations of Nature's handiwork."

"Yes." Sigonio scans the studio, as if he were looking for a chair, brushes an imaginary particle of dust from his lace cuff. "Yes." He barely looks at the canvas. "Fine work, indeed."

Now that Mama is recovered and able to come downstairs more, Father's pride in Vini extends even to his treatment of his wife. He is, if not jovial, positive; if not intimate, gracious. "You see, Antonia?" he asks one night at supper. "You see how God gives even as He takes?" He whisks her mother's full plate from in front of her and replaces it with one of Vini's sketches. "There." He points to the picture, his arm blocking most of her view.

"If you had blessed us with a son, he could not have drawn this with more skill."

He has spoken matter-of-factly, with only a hint of arrogance. Yet the words are echoing like God's thunder in Vini's ears. It is hard to understand why the walls do not collapse at the sound, why the table still feels solid under her hands. This is so much more than *justo,* more than *buono.* These words are, in fact, exactly the ones Vini has dreamed of her father saying. Yet here they all sit, calm as stone saints, while the glorious words ring out around them.

If you had blessed us with a son. What do you wish for after the greatest happiness is yours? *He could not have drawn this with more skill.* You wish for someone else's. Full to spilling, Vini's eyes find her mother's. Antonia will never mention the baby without her consent, so it is up to Vini.

Part of her would like her mother to keep silent forever. She would like the days to stop rushing ahead, would even like them to curl back on themselves, undoing the gentle swelling of Mama's belly, leaving the altarpiece and the paintings in the studio unfinished so Vini could work on them over and over.

But that is impossible; time will not stand still, and the sun will rise day after day. The baby will grow until everyone notices and it is too late to keep him a secret, a hidden smile between his mother and his sister.

"I do not know much about these things," Antonia tells Prospero, touching the edge of Vini's drawing with one tentative fingertip. "But I am glad that our daughter's work pleases you. I have seen that she has a way with a needle, and so—"

"A needle is not a brush, my good woman." Prospero whisks the picture away, though he fails to replace it with Antonia's uneaten dinner. "In fact, I hope you will make sure our daughter no longer wastes her time with such trifles. We must save her eye and hand for what matters, eh?"

"Yes, my dear." Antonia stands, abandoning her meal. "I will help in any way I can." She looks again at Vini.

"Father." Vini watches him, or rather the curve of his back bent over her painting. "I hope you will allow me to use my needle at least once more. I want to help mother stitch some tiny clothes, some blankets for the baby."

"Baby?" Prospero is still studying Vini's drawing, does not even look up.

"Yes, my dear." The Madonna smile is back on her mother's face. "I am with child."

Vini wills her father to turn and look, to see how beautiful Mama is. But he does not.

"I have waited to tell you until I was certain," Antonia explains. "But Silvana assures me this babe will be a boy, and—"

"That foolish hag?" Prospero turns to face them, angry now. Or hurt, as if an old wound has opened and begun to bleed. "She has been sure before."

He stares at Antonia, first her face, then her hands folded like a lotus over her belly. The vexation is back, the color drained from his face. "It will come to nothing." He strides toward the door. "It always does."

Vini remembers Silvana's dark forebodings, her predictions of disaster and doom. Yet blessing after blessing has tumbled into her family's laps—first her mother's baby, then Prospero's commission in Florence, now Vini's work in the *bottega*. Her father is right. The old Gypsy sees nothing but her own fears. God keeps the Fontanas protected; they do not need herbs or toenails or cards that turn life and death upside down.

Antonia follows her husband into the hall, plucks at his sleeve. "Please, my dear." Her touch is too light to hold him. "This time I am sure. You will have a son. I have prayed to Saint Margaret."

Vini remembers her mother's joy the night she confided the news, her hopeful vision that the baby would mean everything to Prospero. But this is nothing like the moment she must have waited for, nursed like a sweet in the back of her mouth all these months.

"When my brother is born," Vini tells her father, following the two of them, borrowing Antonia's dream, making it hers, "I hope to sketch him. I am sure he will look like a cherub." She takes her mother's hand, tries to bring back the lost smile. "Or the Sweet Babe Himself."

"You may hope all you want, Daughter." Prospero stops, turns to face them, his great dark head featureless in the glow of a torch on the wall behind him. "Hope will not open your mother's womb. She is as barren as the fig tree Jesus cursed on the road from Bethany."

"And when he is older," Vini takes her mother's other hand now, rubs it between hers, "I will teach him to draw. He needs to start early, so that he—"

"Enough!" Prospero is nearly yelling now, pointing at Vini. "I will hear no more."

When he turns again and walks away, grabbing the torch from its bracket and carrying it with him down the hall, it is Vini, not her mother, who weeps, dabbing ferociously at her eyes so Antonia will not see.

The baby is not mentioned again. Except in brief, whispered conferences between Vini and her mother. Yet these strange, dreamy exchanges have begun to make her brother real to Vini, make him sprout, like a tiny seedling in her own heart. Antonia has taken on a sweet and unexpected plumpness, her cheeks filling out, her breasts swelling. Without a word, she compels attention, bringing ripeness and promise into any room she enters. Ripeness and shining eyes that say, to anyone who looks, this time will be different.

And perhaps it will. Now that Vini knows her father believes in her and most certainly does not believe in her brother, all her resentment has dissolved. Sometimes at night, as she slips into sleep, she imagines teaching the little one to mix colors. "No, 'Pero," she scolds. "Not like that." She takes his fat baby fingers and wraps them around the brush, one by one. "Like this. Just like this."

Father continues his lectures most mornings, gathering the

students together, talking about draperies one day, the rigors of anatomy the next. When they use live models, he banishes Vini to the house, but always sends a book with her so she will not suffer from her momentary exile. On her return, he asks her what she has learned and makes her show him. "Yes," he will say, nodding. Or, "Not quite. Do you see here, where the anklebone throws a shadow?" She nods, reworks her sketch, and then resumes her place at the altarpiece.

The chill of winter begins to ease and the work for Florence is nearly finished. Vini is putting the last touches on one of the birds' wings when the fever starts. At first she keeps working, using a tiny brush to lay gray and black feathers over the white form that floats like a dove-shaped hole in the sky. She wipes hair from her burning face, convinced the warmth will pass once Paolo has opened the window. But it does not.

Soon her throat and neck are stiff and aching, her eyes are filled with phlegm, and a dull, insistent pain has wrapped itself around her hips and spine. "Did you hear me, Signorina?"

It is the Ox peering, with a look that is very nearly solicitous, from behind the altarpiece. "Are you ill?"

In truth, Vini has not considered this possibility. But Ludovico's expression and his unusually gentle tone force her to consider it now. "Perhaps," she tells him, trying to rise, her knees made suddenly of water. "Perhaps I need to lie down."

She does not remember falling, she does not remember being

carried into the house. What she does remember is waking to the wet, raspy kisses of Cesare and to the sound of someone softly sobbing.

"Mama," she says. "It is nothing. I only need to rest a little." She tries to prop herself up with one arm, but finds her head is much too heavy to lift to a sitting position. "Then I will finish the bird's wing." She sinks back onto her pillow as the dog, his sharp-clawed front feet on her chest, resumes his damp attentions to her face.

"You and your father!" Antonia shoos Cesare away and pulls a sheet and blanket over her daughter's arms. Instantly Vini is swamped with heat and pushes them off.

"He insists you will be back in the studio tomorrow. He says you will not let woman's frailty keep you from work."

"He is right, Mama." Again Vini tries to sit up, and again she finds she is not able even to turn on one side. "Remember when catarrh set me to coughing and crying at the same time two winters ago?"

Antonia's new plump face dimples, even as the tears are drying on her cheeks. "And you kept asking for water till I thought you would burst like a dam?"

Vini nods. "The coughing, the fever, the thirst. It was all gone in a week." She rubs her runny eyes, then flings off the sheet her mother has replaced. "This will pass even more quickly. It must, I do not want someone else to finish my work."

"But that was different." Her mother is not smiling anymore, and her eyes threaten to spill over again. "It is not the same at all." She touches Vini's burning head, pulls her hand away. "Your fever was not this bad, and besides, you were not covered with these"— she pauses, surveying her daughter with dismay—"these awful spots."

"Spots?" Cesare, undaunted, has scrabbled up the sheets again and is burrowing into the tiny cave of Vini's armpit. She scratches his head and then she scratches her nose and eyes. "What spots?"

"This is not catarrh," her mother decides. "See?" She plucks up her daughter's hand and holds it out so Vini can see. "They are everywhere."

Sure enough, Vini's arm and wrist, even the back of her hand, are covered with tiny red dots. Dots that itch.

"Morbillo," her mother says. Measles. "Beatrice's Giovanni had this. And Daniela as well." She pulls the sheets over Vini for the third time. "Only they were much younger. I do not care how angry it makes your father, I must ask Silvana what to do."

Antonia stands, scoops up Cesare, who offers a single indignant yelp of protest, then starts down the back stairs.

"Mama." When Vini calls after her, Antonia turns.

"Could you close the shutters, Mama," Vini asks, pressing her palms over her face. "The light hurts my eyes."

Chapter Fifteen

VINI'S ROOM IS IN TWILIGHT, EVEN THOUGH OUTSIDE, THE EARLY spring morning is chilly and bright. The physician Father finally sent for has insisted that all her shutters be closed. Yesterday he filled a vial with urine from her chamber pot and used a small blade to scrape ooze off the red spots on her arms and face. Today he is back, and when her mother leads him into the room, the two of them stand like vague ghosts beside her bed.

The doctor has brought a jar of leeches with him this time and a small black veil for Vini to wear over her face. "You have rubbed your eyes so hard they are swollen," he tells her, tying the fabric too tight behind her ears. "This will keep out the light and your fingers as well."

He binds her arm with a cloth, and Vini is glad she cannot watch as he lifts one of the hideous wormlike creatures from the jar. Shuddering, she feels the leech explore her wrist with its clammy, determined mouth.

"Ai," she says as the tiny surgeon cuts into her flesh.

"It is no worse than a small bee sting," the doctor tells her. "Soon your arm will be numb."

Vini feels her mother's hand on her forehead, hears the querulous rustle of Antonia's skirts. "She has never been bled before, Sir. When she was last sick, we gave her only compresses and tonics."

"If all illnesses required the same treatment, Signora," the physician replies, "there would be no work for your humble servant." There is a bow in his voice, but none in his waist, since he is already leaning over Vini. "This will help to draw out the heat and the poison in her blood," he says. "It will not take much time. No longer than morning prayers."

But it does not feel like prayers, the pressure of the leech's invisible teeth. It makes Vini think of bees and flies and needles. And then, because that is not helping at all, she thinks of Cesare's tongue, wet and hard, scrubbing, scrubbing. Or a slug in the herb garden, crossing and recrossing the lettuce.

As soon as the leech is removed and the doctor has gone, Vini peeks from under the veil. Her eyes are so puffed and rheumy that she can see only pieces of light and dark and, up close on her wrist, a small red cross where she has been bled. She lies back while her mother fusses over her, pulls up the sheets, pours another cup of the thick, foul-smelling tea Silvana has brewed.

"This has an odor like a horse stall, but it helped 'Trice's boy."

Antonia slips her hand behind Vini's head, lifting her to the cup. "Maybe if you hold your nose?"

But the taste is every bit as bad as the smell. Vini gets no more than a sip down before she is nauseated and turns her head away.

"One more taste?" Her mother lifts her again. "You will need your strength for your visitors."

"Visitors?" Vini forces down most of the tea, then pushes the cup away. "Is Father coming? He promised yesterday."

"*Sì,*" Antonia says. "And one of the students, I think." She replaces the cup on a chest by the bed, then holds out her hand to Vini. "If you will allow me to dress you, my lady?"

For the first time since she has been sick, Vini thinks about her appearance. She pushes herself to a sitting position, then runs her fingers through her hair. It feels like Cesare's coat after he has been on one of his adventures in the woods. What if Paolo sees her like this? For it must surely be Paolo Father is bringing!

After her face is washed, she begs to leave the veil off. "Only for a bit, Mama," she assures Antonia, angling her head just so, using the smile that always works. "Only until they have gone."

So when Prospero walks into the room, although she has not been able to see more than a watery shadow in the mirror, Vini knows that her hair has been combed until it shines, that her wrists and ears are perfumed with rosemary oil, and that her nightshirt is covered with a pale blue robe. "Papa," she says as soon as his unmistakable girth is standing by the bed. "I have been pining for news of the studio."

"Then news you shall have," he tells her. He does not embrace Vini, as her mother did, does not even touch her. He sits on a chair Antonia has drawn up, barely moving, so far as Vini's clouded eyes can tell. "In fact, I have brought you a fellow student to help me report the latest marvels." He turns now. "Come, Sir. Come in."

There is a moment, as the shadowy form crosses the threshold and strides toward the bed—perhaps a few heartbeats— when Vini thinks the other visitor is Paolo. But then the stocky shape arranges itself into a familiar profile, and when it speaks, the disappointment burns through her like a new fever. "Are you well, Signorina?" the Ox asks. "Will you be able to return to us soon?"

Ludovico's voice sounds softer than usual, genuinely concerned. Perhaps her fainting the other day has scared him into compassion. Or perhaps he is a gifted counterfeiter, this unctuous tone an act for her father.

"Father's physician has taken all my blood," she tells them, only half joking. "But as soon as my body learns to walk without it, I will rise up and finish the altarpiece."

"But . . ." The Ox hesitates, and Vini can picture him shifting from leg to leg, looking to Prospero for guidance. "The altarpiece is already installed, Signorina. That is why Master Fontana asked me to visit you." Another pause, perhaps another glance at his teacher. "I am the one who finished it."

Of course! Vini's poor bird is flying with wings the Ox has given it. How Ludovico must have savored each brushstroke. How he must have relished "correcting" Vini's mistakes, "improving" her work.

"The church fathers are delighted," Prospero tells her. "They will be commissioning a fresco for the sacristy and paintings for two more altars."

"Your work was nearly perfect, Signorina," Ludovico adds. "Your little bird was so daintily rendered, it needed only a few touches to soar."

Again, the voice is gentle, sincere. Crafty or contrite, Vini cannot say. She knows only that hating this young man, being suspicious of his every word, is exhausting. It is less trouble to sigh, to turn to her father with the question she has wanted to ask for days: "Papa, can I have some drawing paper? And some pencils?"

As if he has known she would ask, Prospero lays a package on the bed. "You are right," he tells Vini, leaning toward her, animated now. "There is no time to waste." She hears, rather than sees, his smile. "Not if you are to help with the bishop's commission."

"More work?" She is hopeful, smiling. "From whom?"

"The bishop wants three portraits, one for each of his sons." Her father's voice lowers, warms with the pleasure of condescension. "Not that any of them needs to be reminded of the old busybody."

Vini cannot hide her disappointment. "They will be indoors, the portraits, no?"

"Of course," Father tells her. He waits only a moment before he adds, "But there will be a window in each of the backgrounds. His lordship insists upon views of his park."

More trees! More clouds! Sketches and studies and colors! The future unfolds once more, inviting her, teasing her. Light through a window with a stained-glass top! It will spread like melted butter, thick and warm. It will make some things soft and uncertain at their edges, yet bring others to life where it squirrels its way into the dark.

"Perhaps I should have Aldrovandi come and work with you?"

"Yes, please." Ulisse with tokens from outside—leaf buds, salamander skulls, sprigs of thistle and pine. Instinctively, Vini glances toward the shuttered windows, sees only a thin ribbon of brightness around each. Spring is shaping itself without her.

"And now we will leave you, Lavinia." Prospero stands, stamps his feet like a nervous horse. "It is my hope that we will be in church together next Sunday, and that you will be back to work in the studio after that."

"Oh, yes, Father. Yes, I will work hard to keep up."

"I know you will. You have not disappointed me." He turns,

walks toward the door. "Come, Carracci, Antonia. Let us give our patient a chance to rest."

The door shuts behind them, leaving Vini in the dark. Alone, she realizes that since her father's news of the portraits she has not thought once about Paolo. Only minutes before, she wanted to cry because her dear friend had not come to visit. But now she is puffed with Prospero's praise, or what amounts to praise for him: *You have not disappointed me.*

I never will, Papa, she promises, opening the package he has left, fingering the pages of paper, the pens. *I never will.*

When the physician comes back, he makes a great show of removing the veil, of throwing open the shutters. But Vini already knows what she will see when he does. She has spent nearly a week hoping it is not true, and another two days crying because it is.

"There now," the healer tells Vini and her mother. "The swelling is down and the Signorina is ready to look at the world."

But there is nothing to see. Instead of getting better, Vini's eyes have gotten worse. Instead of separating into distinct shapes and colors, as the doctor assured her they would, the patches of light and dark have faded, first into a gray haze, then into a long night from which she cannot wake.

"Give us a kiss, Vini." Her mother is too happy to notice Vini's silence, her sodden posture in the bed. "At last we will be able to take walks in the garden! There are no flowers yet, but there are tiny buds and the trees are full again."

She pulls Vini to her, then pushes her away. "Why, what's the matter, my love?"

Vini has kept her awful secret until now. When her family have visited, they have found her, veil in place, dutifully waiting for her day of release. "I cannot see," she tells her mother. It is a relief to say it at last.

Over and over, each time she is alone, or perhaps snuggling with Cesare, she has lifted the veil, a cautious corner first, then the whole black prison. Each time, she has seen what she sees now: satin darkness, the impenetrable lining of a great dark cape. "I can see nothing at all," she says again.

"Of course you can," the doctor tells her, his voice dispassionate, even. "It will take time to become accustomed to the light. Then my lady will find all that is dear to her."

"No." Vini feels the panic mount as she realizes he is wrong, as she turns hopelessly from side to side. "I tell you, I see nothing."

She hears his consternation, his alarm. "Perhaps you need to wear the veil a while longer." The doctor is already retying the hateful cloth, pulling the cords back into the raw grooves they have dug in the skin behind her ears. "Perhaps we should wait before we summon your father."

When Prospero left her the paper, Vini tried to draw. But she had barely been able to see her hand, a dull, foggy shape moving across the glowing page. Later, even the light of the paper had dimmed, and nothing stood out at all. Now she no longer tries. It is like shedding a sin, like confession, to tell them again, "It is no use. There is nothing but black."

They do the only thing they can: they wait. For a day. Then another. And another. The physician tries poultices of fennel and crushed tomatoes, spreading the juicy bundles on her eyes and forehead, cautioning her to lie still and pray or recite her lessons while they work. Silvana brings a bowl of water in which she has soaked a coin and some grass, then places the damp blades across Vini's eyes. Antonia sits by her bed, stitching and praying to Saint Lucy.

"Santa Lucia," Vini hears the words over and over until they blend together, "intercede," "perfect sight," "honor and glory." As Mama prays, Vini remembers pictures of the beautiful martyr, carrying the eyes her torturers plucked out before they killed her. In every picture, the eyes rest on a shallow dish that Lucy carries as if she is offering the viewer a rare delicacy.

They have lids and lashes, those lost eyes, and they stare, open wide, from the blue plate. Vini wonders what they saw, the saint's eyes, when Lucy died. When she shuddered, then drew her last breath, did the world go suddenly black? Or did the light leave slowly, dark descending bit by bit, like the soft fatal paw of a panther, like the blackness Vini wakes to each morning?

She tries not to think about the future—a future without sight.

She calls back Paolo's face, pictures him behind her closed eyelids. She tells herself that he has not visited her because he is too busy, too sick, too anything besides afraid of her helplessness.

And the studio. She must not worry about that, either. Must not go stiff with anxiety over the number of altarpieces that will be finished without her. Or the apprentice Father will find to take her place if she can no longer paint.

But perhaps Prospero has already given up hope. He has stopped coming to see her, though Antonia begs him to. "He says he is too busy," her mother reports. "He has no time for us or for church anymore." She pauses, then tells the hardest part. "Yet he has time to stay up all night in his study. He sits and stares at nothing."

"Nothing?"

"When I ask if I should have Betta make up a bed for him by the hearth, he does not answer. Only mutters about God and the Fontana name."

If God has punished Papa by denying him a son, then Vini supposes it is no wonder He has struck his daughter blind. For the briefest of months, Father was different, more alive, kinder. But now it seems he has found comfort in his old habit of despair.

Vini, too, feels hope slipping away. "If only I could draw, Mama," she says. "If only I could feel a pencil in my hand." *Without the studio, how will she be who she must?*

"But you *can* draw." Antonia, as if Vini has asked for a drink of water or a spoonful of soup, fetches the paper. "Here," she says, forcing a charcoal stick into Vini's clenched fingers.

Vini hears her own laugh, hollow, resentful. "Like this?" she asks. "I cannot even see the page."

"I will tell you when you come to the edge," Antonia says, as if she is saying, "Here, take a sip."

"Mama, how can you talk like this? I need eyes to draw." Her father's words, the words she has heard for years, haunt her now: *Draw first with your eyes, garzoni.*

"Remember Camilla, the youngest of Betta's girls?"

Has her mother chosen now to gossip? Vini's useless eyes fill with tears. She sniffs against the sleeve of her shift.

"She has one leg that drags behind her."

"Mama . . ."

"At Carnival last year, I saw her dance a jig."

"Mama . . ."

"There!" Antonia's voice is soft as a light in the hills, a light carried by someone far away. "You have already drawn something." She takes Vini's fingers and runs them across the page where Vini has been pressing the paper in her distress. "It looks like a nest, a small, messy nest." She pauses. "We will have to ask Ulisse which bird makes such careless nests, eh?"

Vini laughs again, less angry, more curious. "Did I really make a mark? I did not mean to."

"It is dark in the center, that nest. Perhaps an egg is there?"

"How could I draw without eyes, Mama?"

"You used your hands, love." Antonia must be smiling because her voice has the same girlish quality Vini remembers from their day in the garden. "And maybe your heart?"

"What would Papa say if he saw my messy nest?" Vini runs her fingers over the spot again, putting them to her nose, then to her lips. She draws some more, this time pressing harder and moving the charcoal as fast as she can. "My big, sloppy, mad, mad nest!"

"Oh, look!" Perhaps Antonia does not notice that Vini's hands are covered with tears; perhaps she sees only their busy dance. "There are curls and loops and tangles everywhere," she says. "I think your bird has found clover and ivy and bits of string!"

"My poor little bird," Vini sobs, unable to stop drawing or crying. "It has no eyes, and even its wings belong to someone else!" When the charcoal breaks, she finds a small stub and mashes it into the paper, rubbing furiously until there is nothing left but powder. "Pray to Saint Lucy, Mama. Pray for my blind little bird."

Even as Vini is swept into her mother's arms, even as she hears the low, keening chant of Antonia's prayer, her fingers keep moving, doing what they are used to, what they know. Though her whole body is convulsed with weeping, she cannot stop her hands from remembering, from flying across the page.

Chapter Sixteen

IT TAKES ANTONIA TWO FULL DAYS TO COAX HER DAUGHTER INTO the garden. Vini has stayed in her room for three weeks. The small, fiery bumps on her skin are gone, the fever is over. "Your face is an angel's again," Antonia tells her. "The doctor wants you to take the air whenever you can."

"And why, Mother"—Vini hears her father in her voice but cannot check the bitterness—"should we listen to that learned fool?" She has done blind drawings every day, has let her mind and heart push lines onto the page. Now she is letting them shape her words, too. "I am a painter without eyes. Can he change that?"

Still, once she is assured no one else will see them, that she and her mother will spend the morning alone, Vini agrees to be guided down the stairs. Every step feels unreal, like the game she used to pay with Ginevra when they were little. They would allow themselves to be blindfolded and whirled around until they stumbled with dizziness. But this time, when she trips on a step, Vini cannot stop the game, cannot tear off the blindfold and hand it to someone else, saying, "Your turn now."

Once they are outside, Vini is distracted from her anger at the doctor and the step. She is suddenly awash in sounds: birds scolding each other, the fountain tumbling and plashing, her own steps whispering across wet grass. And even colors! Not colors that form shapes, that have names and build the world, but watery shadows that dance in front of her as they walk. It is a relief from the total blackness, the panther's paw that has covered her eyes for so long.

She has thrown the hateful veil away and can see, at least, hints of what she is missing. The sun and the branches overhead, the fountain—she cannot pick them out but she senses their life, their movement. It is as though they are just behind a gauzy curtain, trembling, waiting. *Closer.* She almost says it out loud. *Come closer.*

In the garden, Vini clings to her mother's arm with one hand, trails the other across the top of the old stone wall. Guided by her nose, she finds a patch of lavender. She runs her hands over the plant, crumbling leaves until her fingers are covered with the familiar scent.

Cesare, invited along on their outing, yelps encouragement as his mistresses spread out a quilt. He dances over and around their hands as they unpack a basket filled with Vini's paper and pens, a jug of wine, and some new pears. "No, bad boy," Antonia tells him. "This is not for you. Go, go and lie down."

Vini settles on the quilt, a spray of lavender in her lap. She does not need to close her eyes for the smell to fill her, to become all there is, everything.

But then Antonia holds one of the fragrant pears between Vini and the plant.

"I am not hungry, Mama."

"But the doctor said—"

"Can we forget about the doctor, Mama?" She inhales the lavender once more, as if she were finishing a meal, then stretches herself full-length on the quilt, her head cradled in her hands, her face to the sky. "Just for today, eh? Let Cesare hunt caterpillars while you and I plan the garden. Let there be no talk of measles or diets or treatments." She shifts away from the knotted braid at the back of her neck, finally sighs and undoes it, fanning her hair out around her. "Please?"

She hears a promising rustle as Antonia pulls her drawing paper from the basket. Cesare rushes to takes advantage of Vini's prone position, nosing through the lavender to push his moist snout in her face. She brushes him away from the flowers, hears him sigh heavily, feels his solid little rump settle against her ankles.

Her mother has sliced a pear, and Vini reconsiders. The scent has made her hungry, not for food but for everything she cannot see. She begs a piece of fruit, rolls it between her hands.

"I know what most pears look like," she says, pressing, kneading, as if there were a secret inside she could squeeze out. "But I do not know how this one is different from the rest." She feels along the skin until she finds a place where it is worn away, where her thumb sinks into the soft, damp meat. "I want to know how every pear looks, Mama. Is this such a great thing to ask?"

"I pray all the time to Santa Lucia," Antonia tells her. "I ask her to restore your sight. When I am with Silvana in the kitchen, I pray. When I am sewing for the baby, I pray."

"I cannot even help you make his blankets now." Vini imagines the tiny sheets and shifts, each trimmed in running stitches, each folded in chests, waiting. She puts down the pear and sits up. Slowly, fingers spread wide, she reaches out her hand and lowers it, timidly, toward her mother's belly.

Antonia covers her daughter's hand with her own, presses it against her gourd-tight stomach. "I have already felt him kick twice today," she says. *"Speta."* Wait. "Maybe he will jump for his big sister."

They sit in silence, the two of them. Vini is patient; she has been rewarded often enough to know it can happen. And yes, after a little time, perhaps the length of a Paternoster, she feels it. It is as if there is a small wave, a crest of water building under her hand. It rises to meet her, pushes so stoutly against her fingers that she can trace its path from one of her mother's hips to the other. And then, brief miracle, it falls away.

"What good will a blind sister be?" she asks, removing her

hand, letting self-pity swamp her. "How can I swaddle him or bathe him? How can I teach him to paint?"

"God will not let you stay in the dark," Antonia tells her. "He sets the stars' courses, but He hears our prayers, too." She sounds so confident, so sure. "Through His grace, you will see your brother's face when he is born."

"But what if Silvana is right?" Vini has forgotten pears and lavender and the crisp, sweet smell of spring. "Her cards foretold darkness." She does not tell her mother the rest of the old woman's prediction, but it lodges like a jagged pit in her chest and throat.

The memory of Silvana's voice, pebbly, frightened, chills Vini now more than when she first heard the old Gypsy's warning: *There will be darkness in this house before the year is out. Darkness and death.*

If Vini's blindness is the darkness, does that mean death is still to come? *Blessed Catherine,* Vini prays against the cards' curse, *please watch over my mother on the day of birthing. If I never see another pear, only keep her safe.*

"Ah, Silvana!" Antonia pours some wine and hands the mug to Vini. "She says first one thing and then another."

Darkness. "Have you asked her about my eyes?" Vini is not certain she wants to hear the answer to this question. But she is equally sure she will know if her mother makes up a lie. Her ears and her heart are bound so tightly now, no one can tell her something untrue without her catching their false starts, their quickened breath. Each time she has asked about Father, her mother has said he will visit her soon. Each time, Vini has known it is a lie.

"Silvana says that your eyes will heal." Antonia's voice is calm, unfaltering. "In fact, she says you will see more than you want." She laughs. "Then, of course, the silly woman carries on about grief and destruction and the fall of the mighty."

"I thought she was wrong, Mama." *May my mother give birth to a sweet, fat cherub of a boy.* "The cards seemed like a joke. I thought we were too happy to fall."

"She likes to wring her hands, that old one." Antonia smoothes Vini's hair from her face, then kisses her cheek. "We will be happy again."

If I never make another painting, only protect Mama, Holy Father, and hold her in Your love.

Cesare, tired of behaving himself, stirs. Vini feels his front paws on her knee, then hears Antonia drop a second mug, hears it shatter against a stone. "Now look what you have done, bad boy!" her mother cries. "I have spilled wine all over my dress."

The dog scampers off, and Antonia opens the basket once more. There is the sound of vigorous scrubbing, cloth to cloth.

"Mama?" Vini is alert, tense as a hound on the scent. "What color dress are you wearing, Mama?"

"The peach-colored one," her mother says, sighing, putting the napkin back in the basket. "With the gold and black vest. Why?"

"I thought so." Vini is more surprised than proud. "I do not see it, but I can feel it." She lets her head fall against her mother's shoulder. "I cannot explain how, but I know."

"I told you!" Antonia sounds suddenly hopeful, touches Vini's arm, runs her fingers down it to clasp her daughter's hand. "Silvana is right. You *are* getting better."

"But I told you, Mama. I did not really *see* it."

Her mother lets go Vini's hand, reaches up to undo the scarf she has woven through her own hair. "Let us put this to the test, Artista."

Laughing, she commands her daughter to sit still. She kisses her forehead, then ties the silk around Vini's eyes. "Now," she says, "which scarf is this, Signorina? Is it my purple with the guinea hens? The green with the yellow stars? Or the blue with oranges and ivy?"

Vini closes her eyes under the scarf, as if she is giving them permission to rest. She imagines Ginevra grabbing her by the shoulders and whirling her around. She does not know how long she sits, how long the swirl of strange, dark patterns swims under her lids. It is as if all the colors there could possibly be are huddled together, like souls in Purgatory, waiting to be free. But then, at last, she feels sure. One color drifts from the shadows, bathes the others in its light. "It is the green, Mama, is it not?"

Antonia kisses her again. "How did you know, minx? It is! It truly is!" She rifles through the basket, ties a new scarf in place of the old. "And this?"

"The blue one," announces Vini. "It is the blue."

"Ai!" Her mother unties the scarf. "Saints preserve us, you are a wonder."

But Vini does not feel like a wonder. Last night she woke in the middle of a dream and, forgetting she could not see her way to the close-chair, walked into a chest, then the wall, and finally collapsed in tears.

Still, there is no denying that she sensed the colors of the scarves. She did not see them, she knows that; her eyes were closed tight. Did she smell them, then? Or suck them up through her fingers? She remembers Father laughing at the beggar reaching for coins on Christmas Eve: *He must have eyes in his fingers, no?*

Vini is feeling sorrier and sorrier for herself, but just when she is about to suggest they go inside, Cesare tears across the quilt between them, growling a challenge at something by the stone wall. "Ohhhh!" Antonia grabs her daughter's arm. "Stay back, you foolish boy! Come away from there!"

The dog has undoubtedly cornered some tiny prey. But it is not a caterpillar; Vini can tell that much from her mother's screams.

"Aiiii! Filthy!" What does Antonia see? Her body is pressed tight against Vini's now, and she is more frightened than angry. "Vile beast!"

"Mama, what is it?" Vini turns toward Cesare's yapping, sees only the shifting of veils, the vague passing of one cloud over another. "What?"

"A scorpion!" Antonia is, standing, pulling Vini up with her. "Sweet Savior, there are more of them. Hideous black monsters!" She puts her arm around Vini, holds her hand. "They must have a nest in the wall."

Darkness and death. Vini is strangely calm. As if she has been expecting such a visitation, as if it is exactly what must follow even the smallest pleasure. She lets go her mother's hand and takes a step toward the wall, not away from it. Her mother tries to pull her back, but she resists.

"Cesare!" Vini pats her skirt, uses a voice the dog knows, a voice that says there is a treat waiting. "Here, Cesare. Come here." *Death and darkness.*

The dog races to her and she grabs his collar. "Show me where they are." Vini's voice promises nothing now, only commands. "Show me."

"Vini!" Her mother rushes to her. "Do not be foolish. You will get bitten."

But Cesare barks and leaps forward, dragging Vini with him. When they reach the wall, she touches it with one hand, takes off a slipper with the other. "Get out!" she yells to the scorpions, to Silvana's cards, to everything that has gone wrong with the world. "Get out of here! Leave us alone!"

She stoops down, beating the ground with her slipper while

Cesare yelps his own threats. "Go back to the dark where you belong! You do not frighten us!"

Vini does not hear Antonia walking toward her; she is too busy pounding, hammering. She imagines a parade of glistening black shells streaming across the ground. Like a pack of lying cards, like an endless string of days as dark as night. Her arm is raised for another furious attack when her mother's voice stops her.

"Come away." Mama sounds as if she is calming a child or a lunatic. "Come away. It is done now. The filthy things have run back into the wall." In the moment that Vini hesitates, Antonia gently takes the shoe from her hand and pulls her to her feet. "It is over," she says.

But it is not over for Vini. When her mother hands her back the slipper, she does not put it on, but uses it to pound the top of the wall, her arm rising and falling in wide, sweeping arcs. She slams the stones over and over until her muscles ache. "Get out! You cannot scare us. Get away, get away!"

When she finally stops, exhausted, Antonia helps her put her shoe on, then leads her back to the quilt. "What a brave one you are," she says, still using her lunatic voice, settling them once more in the sun. "To chase those monsters."

"Mama, I may be blind, but I know scorpions are no monsters." Panting, Vini fends off Cesare, who is trying to sniff out the bit of cake or sweet he is certain he has earned. "They are not much bigger than this." She holds up her index finger, turns it from side to side.

"Small or not, we must have Giorgio kill the pests before someone gets stung." Antonia does not say it, of course, but Vini knows she means before a helpless blind girl steps on one.

"My father was bitten by a scorpion." Mama is always telling stories of Grandfather, but Vini has never heard this one before. "His foot puffed up like a fall melon."

Cesare, deprived of his reward, is darting back and forth between the two of them. "You will get nothing from me, you naughty beast," Antonia tells him. "Go lie down and leave us alone."

"What happened to Grandfather?" Vini, still breathing heavily, thinks to offers a slice of pear to the dog. Cesare devours it, then sits on his haunches beside her, waiting for more. "Did he fall ill from the sting?"

"Crazy old man," her mother says. "He claimed it cured his gout. Still, he had to say novenas for a whole year to atone for the oaths he swore when the thing bit him!"

Grandfather paid a small price, Vini decides. She, too, would be willing to spend a year in prayer if only she could see those black demons with her own eyes. If only she could stand above them and crush each one with her shoe, grind them into powder, hit them again and again with all her strength.

Chapter Seventeen

THEY HAVE FINISHED THE SINGLE MUG OF WINE AND REPACKED the basket when Vini feels the noon sun cooled by a shadow, hears a familiar voice above them.

"Forgive me, Signora," Paolo tells Antonia. The shadow moves and the warmth of the sun is back. *Has Paolo bowed low? Is he kissing Mama's hand?* "I risk interrupting your picnic to ask how Signorina Lavinia is faring."

"I will let you judge for yourself, Signore," Antonia says as Vini reaches up to hold out her own hand.

"Signorina Lavinia is out of bed, good Sir," Vini tells her friend, trembling at the pressure of his hand on hers, then his lips. "But as my father has probably told you, I cannot see well at all." *How must she look, staring blindly toward him? She has undone her braid and her hair is loose, flying everywhere.*

"I am so happy to see you outside, Little One—" Paolo pauses, embarrassed by his slip. "—Signorina," he corrects himself, holding her hand only a little longer than is proper. If Paolo is horrified by her wild hair, her unfocused eyes, his tone does not betray it. His voice is ripe and fond.

"I am going to take my meal in town, and I was wondering—"

Vini does not care what words Paolo speaks, she wants only to keep him talking, to let that dear voice wash over her.

"That is to say, if you are not too tired—"

"*Si?*" She wonders why she has never noticed before how rich his voice is, deep and plum colored.

"I was hoping you and your good mother would allow me to escort the two of you to town this afternoon."

"To town?" What can Paolo intend? Why would he want Vini, half blind and fresh from bed, to walk into town?

But now she hears the smile, the eagerness behind his words. "There is a new puppet show today." He pauses again. "I thought that perhaps the Signorina would find it amusing, that it might take her mind off her recent illness and—"

"What did you say? A puppet show?" Antonia is following a trail picking up bits and pieces that make a whole, that gentle her voice and leave it almost as excited as Paolo's. "The little theater that comes to the square? The one that sets up after the noon meal?"

"*Si*, Signora." Paolo is oblivious, but Vini can hear the sly, happy triumph in her mother's voice.

"Ah!" Antonia reaches for Vini's hand, the same one Paolo has just released. "It is a shame that Lavinia has never seen the puppets." She pauses, gives the hand a squeeze. "It seems she is always sleeping in the garden when they perform."

Vini is both embarrassed at being found out and proud of how clever her mother is. A fuzzy, not unpleasant confusion heats her neck and the backs of her ears.

Paolo hesitates. "Yes," he says, committing himself only to the role of echo. "It is a shame, indeed."

"But this can be remedied, no?" Antonia stands and gently pulls Vini up with her. "And why not today?"

"But Mother, I cannot go, I . . ." Her mother is as mad as Paolo.

Antonia sounds hopeful, light and girlish. She turns to Vini and slips her daughter's arm into Paolo's. "Of course you can. Besides, you need the exercise. The doctor says—"

"The doctor again? Mama!"

"Alas, Signor Zappi, I myself am much too tired to attend. Now that I am with child" —she cannot hide, her pride, even now—"every little thing seems to exhaust me."

"I will stay, too, Mama. You need—"

"But I am certain that with your guidance, Lavinia can make her way to the square safely, no?"

"But Mama, I would rather go another day." She is not ready, she cannot face outsiders like this.

"Come, you wicked boy." It is as if her mother has not heard her at all. Cesare yelps contentedly as he is scooped up. "It is time for your nap.

"And Signore."

"*Si*, my lady?" Paolo must be bowing again; the sun is full on Vini's face.

"Do not let my daughter fall. You must hold her close at all times." There is a feather of laughter at the edge of all her words. "Can you do that, Signore?"

Vini feels Paolo straighten, feels his hand wrap around hers. "Yes, Signora, I will keep her safe."

And so, without a word from her, it is settled. Vini is being led like a dog, a blind dog. She tries to keep up, finds herself tripping with every other step. Paolo slows, adjusts his pace to hers, and somehow they manage to walk past the fountain, through the gate, and into the afternoon laziness of Bologna at repose.

As she listens to their footsteps along the cobblestones, Vini lets her escort chatter away about the show, the studio, his happiness at being with her. Instead of catching his delight, though, she grows more dispirited and resentful with every step.

"Why did you not come to visit me?" She might have come at her question obliquely. She might have agreed that the day is warm, might have asked about the show in the square. After all, her work with the apprentices has taught her how to be modest and sly. But she is not with the other students now, or with her father or her teachers. Paolo is different, he has to be.

He stops in the street, takes her hands in his. "I wanted so much to see you, Little One. I thought of nothing else."

Vini remembers the dark days and nights, the waiting, all without a word from Paolo. "Even the Ox came," she tells him, not caring how selfish, how petulant she sounds.

"Your father said that you were too ill for more visitors. He assured us it would tax you." Paolo's voice trembles now, and there is just a hint of anger, a touch of indignation. "He never told us about your eyes."

"He said nothing?"

"No, Little One."

Vini thinks of the Christmas Eve beggar again. She remembers the way Prospero treats slow students and thoughtless puppies, his impatience with mistakes, with imperfection. Of course, why hasn't she realized it before? "Papa is ashamed of me."

"He is not ashamed." Paolo puts his arm around Vini, strikes out again toward town. "He is afraid."

"Afraid?" The idea is preposterous. Paolo does not know Father the way Vini does.

"*Si*. He is afraid of losing you."

Vini says nothing, but she knows better. Prospero Fontana is not afraid of losing anything, certainly not a poor blind girl who must follow Paolo, must be led along like an old woman or a child.

As they near the square, Paolo holds her closer, steers them through alleys and around clumps of people she can hear talking and laughing as they pass. Vini wonders what she and Paolo must look like to them. Do they suppose the girl with the uncombed hair and the clumsy gait is sick in her head?

To hold Paolo's hand, to walk to town beside him with her mother's blessing—how happy this would have made her only a few short weeks ago! But now she is tripping after him, nose held high, blind eyes turning, turning toward hints of light. Is this what her life will be? Is this Our Savior's plan?

And how long will Paolo be willing to guide her like this? How long before he dreams of a girl who can bring a spoon to her mouth without losing half its contents along the way? Who can cross a room without bruising herself on chests and chairs and the cruel corners of tables? He will grow to hate her mincing steps and her hands, always poking, prodding, groping.

When they reach the square and stand in the middle of the laughter and applause, Vini grows sorrier for herself still. Yes, she can hear the songs and the long, overblown declamations of the puppets; yes, she can hear the cries of the vendors hawking knives and bread and cloth. But behind the sounds, taunting her with their nearness, are all the things she remembers but cannot see: the glint of light on the jeweled costumes, the tiny bright robes and the tasseled curtains; the scenery unrolling across the stage, the dances and acrobatics of the puppet people whose stories have pulled her to the square month after month.

Instead of following the action onstage, feeling the excitement mount as the puppets race madly after one another, Vini must wait, ignorant, unsmiling, until Paolo tells her everything, paints the colors, describes the dancing, spells out each bow and caper.

It is not another play about Orlando today, and it is not the Duke of Mantua. Instead the puppets are performing a comic tale about a princess carried off by a dragon. Paolo informs Vini that the princess's dress is the color of goldenrod and that it is trimmed in purple. He says her little shoes are pea green and that, when she rides on the dragon's plated back, she kicks its sides as if it were a horse, then waves gaily to the audience.

"Farewell to castle walls," a tripping falsetto sails out over the square. "Farewell to smiles and curtsies. To spinning and studying and being good."

A princess forced to learn sewing and read books, Vini thinks, has little reason to complain. If only she could see to stitch one pillow for the baby. If only she could read the pages of a single book!

Paolo tells her that another puppet has taken the stage and is chasing after the princess and the dragon. "I am sorry to say, Little One"—she can hear the smile in his voice—"that this prince is dressed in a cape far too big for him and a hat feather that is longer than his sword."

"I am coming, my treasure!" Vini hears the puppet prince cry. "I am coming to save you!"

But rather than rescuing the princess, Paolo reports, the bumbling prince gets tangled in his finery and then in his own strings. Around them, the crowd cheers him on. Behind them, in back of the square, Vini can still hear the hawkers announcing how sweet their peaches are, how perfect their salted trout or marzipan. Puppets, fish, golden almond dough—she aches for the sight of them all.

Paolo's voice and the show go on and on: "Now the dragon and the princess are dancing together, Little One. The princess has lost her crown, but she does not seem to miss it. Now the prince is racing toward them. His sword is drawn, but he is carrying it as if it is too heavy. The tip is pointing to the ground. He will wound only grass!"

When he laughs, Paolo leans away from her, as if he is afraid he will offend her, as if he is ashamed to be enjoying himself. But in fact, his loose, gentle laughter is one of the few things that does not make Vini want to weep with loss. She settles into it like a warm nest, like sinking in down.

"Oh!" Paolo squeezes her hand as the audience claps and stomps and hoots. "Now we have trouble!" The hoots turn to a roar. "Look behind you!" a man next to them yells. "Turn around!" others shout.

"What is it?" Vini asks. "What has happened?"

"There is another dragon, Little One. It is sneaking up behind the prince." He laughs, this time forgetting to turn away. "It is twice as big as the first one." Then Paolo is quiet, and the intruder roars its lines:

"Where is my baby?" The new dragon's voice is high and fierce at once. "What have you done with my beautiful dragon child?"

"Ah," Vini whispers. "It is the mother, no?"

"*Sì*," Paolo says, "and it is angry."

"Help! Help!" screams a thin voice.

"That is the princess," Paolo explains. "She is running away from the baby dragon. She is clinging to the prince."

"Save me!" wails the thin voice. "Save me, noble sir."

The battle that follows is full of bloodcurdling shouts and the tinny clash of armor and scales.

At last, the big dragon fells the prince with its tail, scoops up its baby, and lumbers off the stage. The dazed prince is revived by the princess's kiss and all ends happily, with more stamping and cheering from the audience and deep bows from all the puppets.

When the puppeteers come out from behind the stage to take their bows and pass the hat, Paolo is amazed. "There are only two men," he says. "Two to make all that noise!"

"That is the way of it, always," Vini says. She remembers the coming down, the plunge into the real world. "Come away," she says. "Let us leave before they fold up the stage."

Paolo drops a coin in the men's hat, then steers the two of them toward the market stalls. He slows his pace, and Vini hears a woman's voice. "Just like the puppets you saw today, Signorina, Signore. Look here."

Paolo stops. "Have you Bradamante?" he asks the woman.

"No, Signore," she tells him. "Only the show today. How about the dragon, Signore?"

Paolo laughs. "You are very good," he says, then tells Vini, "You should see the way she can move the tail, Little One."

"Or the princess, Signorina. She looks just like you, eh?"

Vini has never held a puppet before. She cannot help smiling as the woman puts the princess into her hands. She feels the thick woolen hair and the gown, puffed with layers and layers of silk. She slips her finger into one of the puppet's hands, feeling the small carved fingers and the hole where the palm is pierced and a string is tied.

"May I have the pleasure of buying you a puppet, Little One?"

"But why?" Vini smoothes the princess's dress, touches the points of her tiny shoes. "I cannot even see it."

"It is to remember today by," he tells her, as his hand tightens around her waist. "One day you will be dancing like this princess. I know it."

"I will not forget today," Vini insists, pulling her finger from the princess's wooden grip, giving back the puppet. "I do not need a present to remind me. But . . ."

Vini remembers her dream, the one in which she is playing with her baby brother, teaching him to paint. How she would like to be a child herself again! Innocent of death and darkness, of strings and puppeteers. "Is there a puppet of the prince?" she asks the woman. She turns to Paolo, touches his arm. "For the baby." For Mama's baby boy. "Would he not love watching it dance?"

She is handed another puppet, but Vini needs to make sure. "What does he look like, Paolito?" she asks. "Is he handsome?"

"He has blue eyes and a fine chin. Yes, handsome, I think."

"And the hat and the cape? Do they make him a fool?"

"This prince fits his clothes," Paolo tells her. "You have chosen well."

She gives the puppet back and the woman wraps it in cloth. When the small bundle is tucked safely under one arm, Vini holds Paolo with the other. *"Grazie,"* she tells him, carefully matching her steps to his. "I will hang our prince over the cradle, so every rock will send him jigging."

At home, in the courtyard, Vini hears the fountain and sighs. "You have been very kind to me," she tells her friend. "Very kind and more patient than I deserve. I am sorry I have not been a better companion."

"You are the only companion I want."

"You had better find another, Paolito." Vini lowers her head, sighs again.

"But why? What are you saying?"

"What if I forget your face?" Her voice catches in a half sob. "What if I have to be led everywhere forever?"

"Little One, do not say such a thing." Paolo draws her close, encircles her. "I would give you my eyes."

"What?" Vini is still picturing her future, imagining herself steered from meals to bed to meals in an endless cycle of dismal days.

"I would give you my eyes, if they could help you see."

Vini hears him now. She abandons the pathetic specter she has called up and thinks instead of Paolo. Of all he has done for her. How he has lied and sneaked; how he has risked the respect of the man he reveres more than any other and the job he wants most of all. "I know," she tells him, finding his eyes and his mouth with her hands, tracing their precious shapes with her fingers. "I know that you would."

Paolo closes his eyes under her touch, then takes her hands in his and holds them to his chest. "I wish *riposa* could last forever, but it is nearly over. I must get back to the studio."

Vini pictures the late sun pouring through the *bottega* window, the rows of drawing tablets, the smell of plaster. "Just a few minutes more?" she begs, knowing Paolo will not deny her. Suddenly this fragment of afternoon, the tender ache in her chest, and the dizzying warmth that rushes into her arms and legs make her feel alive. She does not want them to stop.

"Of course." Paolo takes her arm and leads her past the fountain. "I know where we can go."

When they reach the stable and hear low, whinnied salutations as they walk past, Vini realizes where he is taking them.

Her mother's tiny garden is filled with memories for both of them, memories of shy embraces and one perfect almost-kiss. It is not long before the new puppet is set carefully on the stone wall and Paolo's arms are around Vini, as if they belonged there, as if they were designed only to hold her.

This afternoon is different. This time, the two of them are swifter, surer in the way they come together, the way Paolo's lips press hers, the way hers melt, open, and then let him inside. This time, Vini closes her eyes, and floats into his kiss as if it were a deep, quiet pool that will go on forever. A place where there is no need to see. Or think. Only drift wherever she is pulled, wherever the scent and pressure of him draws her.

She has forgotten about puppets and babies and darkness. She is pressed against the wall, clinging to Paolo as if all that matters is this sweetness, this fall, this burning—"Ai!" she screams as the fire pierces her heel. "Oh, oh, oh." Her hand is on her mouth now, and she is hopping from one foot to the other, breathing hard and fast. "Oh, oh!"

"What?" Paolo tries to grab her hands. "Have I hurt you? What is wrong?"

"Ai! I have been stung!" Vini tears off her slipper, rubs the foot that smarts and tingles and itches all at once.

Paolo falls to his knees. "Here, let me see." He holds her foot, touches the heel where it is already swollen.

"Ai!" Vini braces herself against the wall, then remembers. "Cesare found a scorpion's nest right here this morning." She stands on one foot, her other cupped in Paolo's hands. "I forgot all about it. I did not think, I . . ."

"It does not look too bad. Does it still sting terribly?"

"Not so much now." She lets him press the spot harder, turn her foot from side to side. When he stands up, he pulls her away from the wall and takes her again in his arms.

"You see?" she says. "I have given you a perfect excuse for being late to the studio." She lays her head on his chest as if it is a pillow and she is planning a very long nap. "Perhaps you should walk me to the kitchen so we can ask Silvana for one of her plasters?"

"Yes." But Paolo makes no move for the garden gate. Instead he stays where he is, his arms circling her. "We must go right away."

"*Si*," Vini agrees. "Just as soon as we have kissed goodbye." She tilts her face up to his and he leans toward her. But then she stops him, one hand on his arm. She stares at the shape above her, at the picture that is sharpening, clearing, like a reflection on still water at dawn.

She stares and stares. She sees two brown eyes looking back at her, two familiar eyes filled with love. She sees the dark arms of trees behind them, and behind those, the endless light of the sky. "Paolo?" she asks, touching his shoulder, as if in a dream. "Paolo, what color cape are you wearing?"

Chapter Eighteen

SILVANA IS CERTAIN THAT VINI'S EYESIGHT WAS RESTORED BY THE scorpion sting. "My grandmother drank a potion of powdered scorpion tail," she announces. "She lived to be eighty-four."

Antonia is convinced the miracle is a direct result of her prayers to Saint Lucy. "I will light candles for her," she promises, "until I die."

Vini herself, however, credits something more worldly. "As soon as you kissed me," she whispers to Paolo, while Betta and Giorgio and the other servants crowd into the kitchen to witness her recovery, "I could see."

"It was not me." Paolo stands close to Vini, his arm laced through hers, forgetting that she can find her way without him now. "God needs your eyes, Little One. Who else can celebrate His world with such skill?"

Coming back to God's world, Vini thinks, is like opening a treasure chest, rifling through precious keepsakes that have been stored away for much too long: her mother's beautiful face; Paolo's russet curls; sunset coating the surface of the fountain; Cesare begging crumbs, twisting in the air like a miniature acrobat; Betta's round, brown arms; Vini's favorite dress with the pearl bodice. It is intoxicating to see them all once more, to savor every curve, every color and texture. And under the delirious thrill of seeing again is a sacred trust, a bond between herself and each thing on which she sets her new eyes: *Pay attention, pintrici. This is your life.*

After Vini has been hugged and fussed over, after Silvana has handed round a clear honey wine with cinnamon and lemon, after Giorgio has drunk to her health so often his speech slurs, Paolo pulls her aside. "Let us go and tell your father now, Little One. He will want to share your miracle."

But Vini makes him promise not to mention the news to anyone in the studio. Not yet. "Let it stay kitchen gossip for now, Paolito," she begs. "I want to tell Papa in my own way." She knows, without being able to say how, that her recovery will be a shock, a surprise only the two of them must share.

So Paolo returns to work by himself, and only after all the apprentices have gone, does Vini visit the *bottega*. She stands at the door, watching her father work in the last light of day, and for a minute she is stunned. He looks so much older than she remembers, moves more slowly and heavily. "Papa," she says, fearing he may be too tired to talk. "Shall I come in?"

Prospero glances up, sees that his daughter is alone. "Wait," he tells her, laying aside his brushes. "I will help you. There is a table in the way."

But before he can meet her, Vini has navigated across the room. She stops a few feet in front of him. "That is not necessary, Papa," she says, unable to hide her joy. "I can see."

He pushes himself up from his stool; standing, one hand still on the easel, he looks at her in silence. It is as if she is a ghost, a vision, something he cannot believe.

"It is true, Papa." Vini turns in a playful circle, curtsies to the portrait of a church elder beside her. "I can see again!"

"No."

"Yes."

"No." And then, "Great God."

Father does not rush toward her, or press her to him, as the rest have done. But in the face he turns to her, Vini sees such change, such a peeling away of shadow, that he is years younger in an instant. He stares at her as if his eyes could drink her up. His expression is new to Vini. It is not relief or even happiness. It is gratitude.

"In all my life, I have asked the Lord for only two things," he says. "Perhaps that is why he saw fit to grant me this."

Father prayed for her! Maybe it was not the scorpion, after all. Or Mama's prayers. Or even Paolo's kiss. It was Father humbling himself to ask God for something. That was the miracle.

Prospero seems shamed by his revelation, stands silent and awkward, as if he has forgotten who they are to each other. *He is better alone,* Vini realizes, only a little surprised. *He was not meant to have a household, a troop of servants, a wife and daughter. He was meant to live like a scholar, existing on words and air.*

"Come here." It is not a command or a request. It is the assumed intimacy of one colleague to another. "I want to show you something."

Vini stands beside him, looks over his shoulder at the large canvas on which he has been working. It is a sketch of Christ with the woman at the well. Behind the two figures, hills rise into a crystal sky.

Other men, other fathers, might welcome their daughters back. They might smile, might weep, might talk of miracles. But Prospero Fontana is not like other men. What he can talk of is not miracles but art.

"Carracci drew this fig tree." Papa points to a small tree clinging to the nearest hill. But he does not look at the tree as he talks. He is looking at his daughter, watching her eyes. Watching her see. "It is not right."

Vini studies the tree: its leaves are too broad, its trunk too smooth and straight. Her lessons with Ulisse have included more than twenty kinds of trees, each with its own leaf shape and bark, its own way of opening to the sky.

Her father speaks without taking his eyes from her, though he still points to the offending flora. "Perhaps you could"—his smile is slight, but unmistakable—"improve it, eh?"

Vini slips off her cloak and steps into the apron he offers. He helps her tie it around her waist, something he has never done before. Vini welcomes this gesture in the same spirit she has accepted the others' hugs. It is the closest he can come.

She sits on the stool he draws up beside his. As soon as she looks at the painting, only half done, Vini comes home. Home to a world where she knows colors before they are born, where she moves without walking, traveling from the picture plane to the background, feeling the light change, the scale diminish.

When her father hands her the palette he has been using, an old excitement threatens to explode like a fireworks constellation in her chest. They are there waiting for her, more delicious than any meal she has ever eaten, headier than Mama's flowers: each color begs to be swept up, mixed, and pressed onto the canvas; each shade will become something new, something never to be repeated, when she has blended, scraped, dreamed it into being.

It will be this way from now on, Vini knows. Every day, she and Papa will work together. He has prayed for her. He has willed this moment into being. Look how, as she coaxes the little tree into bloom, he leans toward her, watches solemnly. Yes, they will work side by side; he promises it with each nod of his great head, each grunt of surprise, each barely discernible smile.

The chain of sweet, full days that follows is doubly blessed. Every afternoon now, after she has painted with her father in the studio, Vini works beside her mother in the little sitting room off Antonia's bedchamber. It is as if she is determined to make up for the time she missed when she could not see; she sews with a fury, turning out blankets and shirts and tiny hats for the baby.

"Not so fast," her mother cautions, laughing. "Your brother can never wear so many!"

One day, they tear sheets into strips for swaddling cloths; the next, they resurrect the wooden walker Vini used when she was an infant, dragging it from a storage closet, straightening its wheels, rubbing it with walnut oil until it shines. They drape the cradle Ulisse has given them with pennyroyal pomanders to keep away fleas, and lay the puppet prince on the tiny satin pillow to see how the baby will fit. "Just right!" Antonia says, holding her belly and rocking the cradle at the same time. "Perhaps we should make Ulisse a godfather, no?"

Some days, Zia and Ginevra visit, and the four of them spend hours in Mama's sewing room, joking, talking, bent over intricate, tiny seams and hems. Before she was sick, Vini was certain there was nothing she would hate more than being forced to sew and gossip. But now every stitch, every word is precious. Her aunt's purring chatter, her cousin's dreamy plans, her mother's silver bell of a laugh; the heaps of linen between them, the spindle, the embroidery hoops, the dying sun angling across their laps. How could she have moved among such things, day after day, and never noticed how beautiful they are?

On one of Zia's visits, Mama remembers the game she and Vini played in the garden. They all take turns tying bright-colored squares of silk over one another's eyes, trying to guess which scarf they are wearing when it is their turn to be blindfolded, while the others yell hints that hardly help at all:

"It is the color of my darling's eyes," Ginevra offers.

"Not at all," insists Zia. "It is exactly the color of the new coat I saw on the widow Cortese last Sunday."

But when it is Vini's turn, she needs no hints, guesses correctly every time. It is as if she is back in the garden again, using her nose, her hands, her silent, waiting heart. She touches the scarf, breathes in, and then it comes. "The gold," she says. "With the grape leaves."

Finally, exasperated, Ginevra calls a halt. "You are much too good!" She unties the scarf from Vini's eyes. "The three of us cannot match your painter's knack."

"Speak for yourself, Daughter!" Zia Beatrice closes her eyes, sits straight and still as a statue. "Try me again. I am sure I can do it now."

Ginevra winks and pulls out a swaddling cloth. Antonia wraps the strip of sheet around her sister's eyes, and Vini invites Zia to tell them what color it is.

"I know! I know!" Beatrice is smiling triumphantly, sure of her guess this time. "It is the blue with the cypress and parrots, no?"

Ginevra and Vini giggle.

"Very well. It is the yellow with the oranges and tigers. I am certain now!" She points to her nose and sniffs loudly. "I can smell the oranges!"

They are all four laughing hysterically when Prospero appears at the sewing room door. He looks in consternation at Vini, Ginevra, and Antonia, then at Zia with the sheet around her eyes.

"Papa," Vini calls to him. "Come try." She sorts through the pile of scarves, hides a green one with angels behind her back. She runs toward her father. "Close your eyes," she commands.

But before she can tie the scarf around his head, Prospero bats her hands away from his face. "I have work to do," he says, his voice brusque, alarmed. His confidence, his calm are dissolved by this roomful of women. "I have no time for foolishness." He hurries out the door and down the hall.

Vini looks after him. For the first time in her life, she feels sorry for Father. For the lovely foolishness he has missed, the silliness, the jokes. All the joy he has pushed away.

Ulisse begins taking Vini on field trips again. As spring turns to summer, her teacher's specimen bottles and Vini's sketchbook fill to overflowing. While it is decided that Cesare is too disruptive, flushing rare birds from hedges before they can be identified, eating leaves and flowers even as Vini is drawing them, there is one companion who is more than welcome to accompany them whenever he can steal a few hours from the studio.

Paolo and Vini do not mean to take advantage, but Ulisse is so deliciously absentminded! He is forever wandering off in search of rocks, then happening on a stream full of mollusks or a meadow of pheasant's eye. Each time, he is gone long enough for so many stolen kisses, tender words, and loving promises that Vini begins to feel as sentimental and lovelorn as her cousin.

She presses flowers between the pages of her anatomy text and saves locks of Paolo's and her hair twined together. She even finds herself, like Ginevra, mooning over her sweetheart when she is not with him. She calls up Paolo's every word and gesture, reliving each moment of their outings with Ulisse, their chance encounters, and their secret meetings in the garden or the music room.

These meetings, though, are rare. Father has taken on five new commissions and has hired more apprentices. He has pulled out the long table in the studio to make work space for a growing army of artists. And if Prospero is this army's leader, Vini and Ludovico are surely his lieutenants.

They work together all the time now, Vini and the Ox. More and more, the two of them are called upon, not only to sketch backgrounds, but to block in central figures in the foreground as well. Though she will never entirely trust the Ox, Vini knows he is among her father's most talented students. She knows she can learn from him. The graceful angles at which he places the people he sketches, the way they turn toward the viewer or come in from outside the picture, as if they are barely contained by the canvas—none of this is lost on Vini. *Take note. Remember this. Never forget.*

Ludovico, in turn, seems to have no more time for cruel jokes or angry words. He is too busy rushing from one canvas to another, his small eyes narrowed, sweat glazing his face. It is hardly even a surprise, then, when one day he comes to her for help. "Signorina," he asks, without a trace of irony, "can you show me how you did those ferns in the saint's cave?"

In between her nature studies and her father's commissions, Vini still uses the little garden shed. But now the hours she steals, the colors she "borrows," are not for a project she hides from her father but for a gift she keeps from her mother. At first, only Paolo sees the birthing tray she is painting, a shallow wooden serving dish with a picture of two women in a garden. "It is lovely, Little One," he tells her. "It will bring the sun inside."

"I know it is not a holy subject, Paolito," she says. "But it is something I have wanted to paint ever since I found Mama's garden." She studies the two figures she has drawn, one standing, the other playing with a tiny dog in the grass. "I want to be the one to bring her first meal after the baby comes. And I want to bring it on this."

⌒∞⌒   ⌒∞⌒   ⌒∞⌒

It is less than a week after she has finished the tray, after she and Silvana have hidden it away behind the grain sacks in the kitchen, that Betta rushes into the studio. It is much too early for supper, and all the servants know better than to interrupt the workday. But Betta opens the door without knocking and hurries to Vini's side, her face flushed, her hands kneading her apron. Everyone in the *bottega* looks up, sees her, and realizes it at once: Mama's time has come. Father glances only briefly from his work, nods at Vini, then, his face set and stiff, turns back to his easel.

Vini does not even clean her brushes. She races with Betta out of the studio and into the kitchen, where Silvana is feeding the midwife's husband. He has accompanied his wife here twice before when Mama felt pains. Twice before, he has wolfed down their food, then returned home with the midwife when it was not Mama's time, after all.

This afternoon the man is so busy stuffing himself with soup and rolls, he does not even look at Vini. But Silvana does. And as soon as the old Gypsy's eyes meet hers, they fall away. That is when Vini knows. Something is wrong.

Chapter Nineteen

AS VINI ENTERS HER MOTHER'S BEDROOM, TWO OF BETTA'S daughters rush out. Camilla, the lame one, and a taller, shy girl whose name Vini cannot remember are loaded with bowls and pitchers and towels. They barely glance at her, their faces flushed and frightened.

The curtains around Mama's bed are drawn back. She is asleep, her face on one arm, her breathing deep and even. Vini feels the gratitude fill her like blood, race to her head. Her prayers have been answered. Mama is fine!

In her mother's other arm, so beautiful it stops her breath, is Vini's brother. The midwife has wrapped him in a blanket, and he is nestled against Antonia's breast. He is not dark like their father; he has blond hair and milky skin, a small angel's mouth. But he is not moving or crying. Vini is certain newborns are meant to be red and full of wiggles and tears.

The midwife, a tall woman with corded arms, puts her finger

to her lips. She has rolled up her sleeves and tied her hair back; even so, her face and arms are shiny with perspiration. "Let Signora rest," she says softly, then leans over the bed, gathering up soiled sheets.

Vini walks, as if in a dream, toward them. She has brought the birthing tray from the kitchen; she puts it at the foot of the bed, her eyes fixed on Antonia and the baby. Her mother's face is lowered toward the little one, but Vini can see the smile, all peace and pride, that lights it even in sleep.

One of the baby's arms has fallen free of the blanket, and Vini looks at the midwife. When the woman nods, Vini reaches out and puts a finger in the tiny hand. His fingers are still and his palm is cold. Without thinking, she covers his hand with both hers, trying to rub it warm.

Leaning close, she sees that the baby's pale skin is touched with blue, not pink. *More ochre in old skin, more rose in young*, Papa has said. But 'Pero's skin, as transparent as a dried petal, is neither.

Perhaps it is the feel of his fingers curled in hers. Or maybe it is the waiting, the hoping, the prayers she has said. During the minute that she holds her brother's hand, Vini sees him, in dozens of tiny visions like stained-glass fragments she picks up, one by one, and holds to the light: there is a picture of her brother in the walker, babbling and rolling after her down the hall; and the image of an older boy, hiding from her in the linen closet, hoping to be found; and later still, Vini and her brother standing with the crowd at the puppet theater, clapping, stamping, laughing until they cry.

But these bits of future are sunless scraps; she cannot make them come clear. All around her, Vini sees things that are sharper, fiercer, more real—the pile of bloody sheets in the midwife's hands, Antonia's face, bleached from exhaustion, this small body that does not respond to her touch.

By the time she stands aside to let the midwife finish, Vini is weeping openly. Her grief, though, is no longer focused on the brother she has lost, but on her mother. Antonia's son, her wished-for babe, her life's crown—is dead.

"I had to wait until Signora slept to take the baby from her," the midwife whispers. "She would not listen to me when I told her it was lost."

"Is she . . . ? Is she well?"

The woman puts her finger to her lips again and shyly takes Vini's arm. "Come, Mistress," she says, and leads them into Mama's sitting room. She urges Vini to sit down, but when Vini refuses, they both stand guard by Mama's door. *"La Signora,"* the midwife explains, "she kept whispering sweet words to the poor dead thing. She held it tight and would not let me take it from her."

She drops her pile of sheets on a chest by the door and sighs heavily. She comes back to Vini, standing so close that her face gives off heat. "So I let her chatter and fuss and kiss it until at last she fell asleep."

"But will she be well?" Vini feels selfish and angry at once. She has lost a brother; she will not, she cannot, lose her mother, too.

"Her body is strong," the woman says, glancing at the door she has only half closed. "As for her heart, that will take time."

"What do you mean?"

"It is hard to give a child back to the Lord before you have even held it in your arms." The woman's lips are dry and cracked, but her face still shines with sweat. "Now I must take the babe, Signorina, before she wakes."

Vini follows the midwife back into the bedchamber. While the woman fetches another blanket, Vini watches her mother sleep. She sees the quiet, bottomless peace registered on Antonia's every feature, the way her whole body is folded around the child. This is not a Madonna from church, with a half smile, a Heaven-directed glance, and a graceful hand gesturing toward her babe. This is a real woman, her hair pressed to her neck in moist curls, her face drawn and damp, holding, holding, holding her dearest dream.

"*Scusi,*" the midwife says softly. "It is time, Mistress." She leans in front of Vini and reaches for the baby.

"Wait!" Vini takes the midwife's hand, pulls her away from the bed. "No." Her whisper is loud, harsh. She cannot bear to see her mother's arms empty, to leave Antonia with nothing to hold. She runs to the cradle in the corner of the room, fumbles among the silk coverlets and pillows. "Here."

Vini scoops up the puppet prince, his lifeless arms and legs dangling, wraps him in a coverlet, and carries him to the bed. "Gently," she warns the woman, who looks at her astonished. "Take him gently."

The midwife does what she has been told, and as she lifts the dead baby from Antonia's embrace, Vini slips the prince into its place. Mama stirs once, then hugs the puppet to her and dreams on.

Vini waits by the bed after the midwife has left with her sad burden. She does not want anyone else to watch Mama's despair. She will be the one beside her mother when she opens her eyes, the one who holds her while she weeps. The birthing tray lies half buried in the folds of the quilt at the foot of the bed. Through misty eyes, Vini sees a piece of the green grass she has painted at its bottom and a dog bounding after a butterfly.

Mama is exhausted when she wakes, exhausted but smiling. "Did you see him?" she asks as soon as she sees her daughter. She shifts the blanketed puppet in her arms, kisses the top of its head.

"*Si*, Mama." Vini moves closer, takes the hand Antonia stretches toward her.

"Is he not beautiful?"

"*Si*, Mama." Her mother's hand is warm and moist. Vini clutches it tight.

"Your father will be so proud." Antonia's eyes are tired but full of quiet satisfaction. "Did I not tell you? Everything will be different now."

"But Mama." Vini will be as patient with her mother as her mother was with her when she was blind. She will lead Antonia back to herself. "Mama, did you not see? The baby is—"

"I know, Love." Antonia's voice is filled with the same calm delight that is in her eyes. "He is everything we hoped."

Vini cannot let go her mother's hand, cannot stop staring at the radiant face before her.

"Your father has waited so long for this day." Antonia glances toward the door as if she expects Prospero to walk through it as she speaks. "You will see how he changes now. How he grows young before our eyes. How he stops pacing and frowning and sitting by himself in the study."

Vini will hold her mother, will smooth her hair, will help her hear the truth. "Mama, the midwife told you about the baby, remember? He is—"

"Hush now," Antonia whispers. "You will wake him." She looks cautiously, tenderly, at the puppet. "But perhaps we should, eh? Will you hold him, Love?" She rises on one elbow, careful to hold the doll close.

Why does she not hear? How can she stare so fondly at that painted toy? Vini feels the tears, the ache in her chest that wants to turn to sobs. "Not yet, Mama." She tries to sound calm and reasonable. "We need to talk, you and I."

Antonia laughs. "Do not worry, silly. He will not break." She holds the puppet out. "You are his big sister. You must learn how to care for him."

Dear Savior, why will she not listen? "Mama, I . . ."

"Here," her mother says, slipping the bundle into Vini's arms. "Only for a heartbeat, then I must have him back." Her eyes do not leave the puppet, and she hangs on Vini's arm while she talks, as though by touching her daughter she is still connected to her precious babe.

"Look how handsome he is." She stares at the puppet, then at Vini. "And look how he loves you already."

Vini lets the tears course down her face. She cannot brush them away. Her hands are full, and she has all she can do to keep from dashing the makeshift babe to the floor and throwing her arms around her mother. *Mama, Mama! Please come back to me. We can be happy again!*

The puppet prince, spineless, inert, stares up at her with a broad smile. *The cards were right, Mama, but they were wrong, too. God steers the stars, remember, Mama? But He also hears our prayers.* The wooden arms and legs make the blanket stick out at awkward angles. The woolen hair, the gold-trimmed cape and hat—all promise to start her sobbing, crying so that she cannot stop. Worst of all, so horrible that Vini needs to bite her tongue when she looks at them, are the strings, streaming in long, lazy loops over her arms and onto the bed.

But Antonia does not seem to notice. As Vini holds the puppet, her mother touches its painted lips, pats its stiff curls. "Perfect," she croons, her voice deep and swollen with love. "He is just perfect."

In the kitchen, Vini tells Silvana and the midwife what has happened. "I have tried to explain that it is only a puppet," she says, "but Mama will not listen." She is vaguely aware of Cesare, yapping at her heels, of the midwife's husband by the hearth, of the two women listening to her. But superimposed over everything, coloring it all, is the memory of her mother's smile, her too bright voice. "We must do something, please!" she begs them. "We must call the doctor."

"No, Preziosa, no doctor." Silvana takes Vini's hand. "Do you want them to keep your mother locked up? Or worse, take her away?" She turns to the midwife now. "Tell her," she urges in her gravel voice.

The midwife leaves her bowl of soup on the trestle, comes to stand beside them. "The doctor, your father, they do not understand a woman's sorrow," she says.

"Giovanna has been a midwife for thirty years. She has seen much, Preziosa." Silvana wipes her eyes with a corner of her apron. "She knows the mind will not hear what will break the heart."

"I have seen women nurse phantom babes," Giovanna says, "seen them sing lullabies to the air. You must give the Signora time. When she is ready, she will hear the truth."

"But when?" Vini asks. "When will she be ready?"

The two older women look at each other. "She will tell you," Giovanna explains. "You will know."

Time. It is a little thing, Vini decides. If time is all Mama needs, Vini can wait. She knows well how Mama waited for her. How she nursed and stroked and soothed her angry charge. How she wept and prayed.

When they all three troop upstairs again, Mama is still awake, the puppet beside her in the bed. She shines her heartbreaking smile at them. "Come in," she says. "Come in and see." She looks behind them, out the door. "Why have you not brought his father?"

"The Master is not with us, Signora." Silvana slips the painted birthing tray from under the covers, places it on a chest by the bed. She stands near Mama now, her hands folded across her chest. "Signora, I am glad to see you so well." She smiles her toothless grin. "From the cries I heard in this room a while ago, I thought surely you were giving birth to three babes at the least."

Mama laughs too loud. She looks at the puppet in her arms, kisses its face. "As you can see for yourself, Silvana, there is only one." She leans toward the toy, whispers something they cannot hear in its wooden ear. "But Our Lord has seen fit to give me one worth three others, no?" Again she glances toward the door. "When is Prospero coming?"

The years of hoping, of losing faith and finding it again. They have swept Mama up, have carried her off. But she will come back, Vini tells herself. Just as Vini recovered her sight, her mother will be restored to her. She must be. Or nothing else, not even painting, will matter.

"Perhaps," Giovanna says, stepping in front of the others, "Signora would like to rest for a while? I have a soothing potion here that will help you sleep."

Before she can pour from the pitcher, though, Mama is sitting up in bed, pushing the cup away. "Thanks, good gentlewoman," she says, "but there is more important business to attend." She looks at the wooden face in her lap. "Prospero Fontana must meet his heir." She looks up and inclines her head toward them, regally, gracefully. This is the moment she has planned for, dreamed of. "Now," she says, "would you be so kind as to summon my baby's father?"

When Vini tells him the sad news at supper, Father closes his eyes for an instant, as if a cinder has flown into one. She notices how slowly and precisely his knife cuts into the meat, how long he chews each piece.

All through the meal, he says little but moves with the leaden, painful deliberation of someone who has been pushed down but who staggers to his feet and moves on. Vini remembers that this is how Papa acted after his student died of typhus. While everyone else was crying and praying, Papa closed his eyes, squared his shoulders as if he were shifting a heavy weight, and went back to work.

After supper, he agrees to go with Vini to see Mama. They have reached the landing when she tells him about the puppet and cautions him to pretend it is alive. The midwife has said this is best, Vini assures him, that Antonia will grieve her loss when she is ready. Until then, she needs her shadow babe.

Papa's face hardens but his eyes seem—what? Can it be fear that makes them brighter, sharper? "I have worked hard from first light, Daughter," he says. "I am too tired to play at puppets." He turns and walks back down the stairs. "Tell your mother I will come another day."

Vini remembers waiting for her father to visit after she lost her sight. She remembers how long it was before she realized he would not come. So Antonia waits, for days, alert to each footfall on the stairs. But it is only Vini and sometimes a servant who come with meals, or to empty the chamber pot. They assure her that her new son is the most well-behaved, loveliest babe they have ever seen. They promise that Prospero is eager to visit, that he will surely come soon.

Vini pets and gossips and soothes. Every day she brings her mother food on the new tray. It is the one thing, besides her painted child, that Antonia continually admires. She has decided it must be framed when her confinement ends. "So lovely, this mother and child," she says each time she lifts her plate to reveal the painting underneath. "I will eat very carefully, eh? I do not dare to spill a drop."

But as each afternoon turns to evening, as the laughter and talk of the departing students drift from the courtyard into her window, Antonia turns restless. She looks from the window to the door. "Why has he not come?" she asks, clutching the puppet. "Does he not want to see his son?"

Chapter Twenty

AFTER THE MIDWIFE HAS COME BACK TO GIVE MAMA A DECOCTION
that will dry up her milk, Zia Beatrice visits. Vini is grateful
beyond words to see with what gentleness her normally loud and
boisterous aunt treats her sister.

"Look at you, 'Tonia," Zia tells Antonia. "You are a vision!
When Vini told me the news," she squeezes her niece's hand, then
sits beside the bed, "I just had to come."

Vini's mother is still smiling, still filled with that strange,
unbending joy, but she wears a new look for her older sister. It is
hope, Vini thinks. Hope that someone, almost as important to her
as Prospero, will witness, will seal her triumph with approval.

Antonia clasps the puppet tight, but turns so that Zia can see
its face. "What do you think, 'Trice?" she asks. "Is he not even
handsomer than his father?"

Zia looks at the doll and, like Prospero when Vini told him the
baby had died, she closes her eyes. She turns just for an instant,

and Vini can see her brush away the tears. When she turns back, she kisses Antonia on the forehead and says exactly the right thing, the truest thing she can: "You have worked so hard, my sweet sister. You deserve the most beautiful bambino in all the world."

When she is able to leave her bed, Vini's mother takes the wooden prince everywhere. If she eats supper in the sitting room, she dines at a small table by the window with the puppet's cradle beside her. If she takes the afternoon air on her balcony, the puppet comes, too, swathed in blankets for fear it will catch a chill.

But without a visit from Prospero, Antonia is an imitation of happiness, a pitiful dream that haunts the house. And the studio, too. Even when Vini escapes for a few hours to the *bottega*, she hears in her head the lullaby her mother croons to the wooden baby. Sees the patient Madonna's grace with which Mama changes its swaddling clothes or puts it to breast.

Every night, Vini sits at the foot of the bed, hoping Antonia is better, hoping the mother she has treasured this past year has been restored to her. But she has not. "*Sì,* Mama," Vini says. "He is a good child. He never cries." "*Sì,* Mama, I will help you bathe him." "No, I do not think he has lost weight."

One day, when her mother is sorting through the tiny gowns they have sewed and put away, Vini is entrusted with the puppet's care. Holding it as she always does, like a real baby, she studies the silly smile, the splayed fingers. What sort of love could transform this frozen toy into a flesh-and-blood child? Vini has used paints and canvas to imitate life. Sculptors work with stone or clay. But Mama has only her dream, her bone-deep, terrible need to please Prospero. It is clear she would rock the air, sing to her empty arms, to keep her wished-for son alive.

Antonia is still bent over the chest of baby linens. *When will this sad game end?* Vini has held this puppet, dressed it in a dozen different gowns, given it pretend baths, kissed it, even changed its diapers. Wait, the midwife says. Wait. She will mend, Zia promises. She will be herself again. *But when?*

Vini is angry. Angry at her own impatience. At her inadequate love. At the wooden toy whose strings dangle across her lap, who will never wake or cry or soil the diapers wrapped around its jointed legs.

She glances again at her mother; Antonia's back is still turned to her, she is still folding and sorting. Frustrated, failing God's test, Vini gives one of the puppet's strings a cruel yank. Its arms jerk up as if it has been surprised. Vini pulls again, tearing the hateful strings, first from one hand, then from the other.

Quickly, she unwraps the swaddling, pulls the string off each of the puppet's feet. She stuffs them all under her belt, and later, in the kitchen, she throws them into the fire. They catch instantly and burn away without a trace.

꙳ꙮꙮꙮ ꙮꙮꙮ ꙮꙮꙮ

If the nights alone with her mother and her puppet brother have been hard, the hardest is yet to come. After six days of confinement, Antonia decides she can wait no longer. "I am feeling so much better," she tells Vini. "Your father must be growing impatient." She ties her shawl around her and slips the puppet into the sling it makes. "I will take supper downstairs tonight so he can see his son at last." Bent on her own destruction, she walks to the mirror and begins plaiting her hair.

"Perhaps you should wait until you are stronger, Mama." Vini imagines her father tearing the puppet from Antonia's arms. *Look, look,* he will say. *What do your eyes tell you, woman? This is a toy, a scrap of wood!* "Maybe tomorrow would be best."

"No, Love. It is high time Prospero Fontana met his heir." Her mother opens the wardrobe. "We should choose my dress, no? And you must tell Silvana to cook something he likes. Lamb, do you think?" Her eyes are burning, her voice charged with excitement. A bird flinging herself at the arrow, she can hardly wait to see the one person sure to break her heart.

After she has told Silvana about supper, Vini goes to the studio. If it were not for Paolo, she would have nowhere to turn. Though they have had very little time by themselves, the mere sight of him sets her at ease, anchors her. When she walks into the studio, she no longer pretends to look anywhere else first. His smile and his calm, sturdy affection shine like a beacon from across the room. How differently she sees him now than when he was her bumbling, blushing Pony!

"Paolito," she tells him, while Prospero and the stable boys are packing a scaffold to take to Imola, "Mama is no better." She would like to touch his hand, to have his warm fingers close on hers. "I miss her so much." She breathes in the comfort of his nearness. "Before the baby, I prayed for her body. Now I pray for her mind."

"The midwife told you it would take time, no?"

"Yes, but I am so afraid for her. She is awake, but she is dreaming." One of the apprentices looks up from his drawing board and sees Paolo and Vini together; he puts his hands on his chest and makes a stupid, lovesick face. But Vini glares at him until he looks away.

"Your father is afraid, too." Paolo wipes his hands on his shop apron, as if he were going to take her hand, but he does not.

"Afraid?"

"*Si,* Little One. If only you could have watched him after Betta came to the shop, the day the baby . . ." He pauses, his eyes full of apology for saying what he must. "The day the baby was lost."

"What do you mean?"

"He was crazed. He did the work of three or four men that day. It was the same when you were sick."

Vini pictures Papa's stiff jaw, the rigid mask of his face beside her bed. "Are you sure?" All his talk of perspective, of proportion, when she hungered for smiles and fond words.

"I was there, Little One. I saw it for myself." Paolo shakes his head remembering. "He worked so that he would not have to think."

Perhaps there is a sorrow of men, Vini decides, a sorrow she cannot understand.

"He stayed in the studio so he would not have to look at what was happening in the house . . ."

And then Prospero is back; talk all over the room stops. The students sit straighter, hoping *Il Maestro* will smell their industry. But over her drawing board, Vini watches her father. And wonders.

As soon as he is seated that night, Papa notices the third place set at the table. He says nothing, only accepts a cup of wine from Silvana and takes a long, considered sip.

Vini waits until the old servant is back in the kitchen, until Prospero has finished, leaned back, avoiding the extra plate. Her mother, it is clear, is not the only one who refuses to see what she does not want to.

"Mama will be joining us, Padre." She tries to keep her tone even, betraying neither hope nor fear. "She is feeling much better." It must be said. It must be told: "She wants to show you the baby."

His dark brows nearly meet. "Your mother is still persuaded that stick of pine is a babe?"

Vini finds her hands in her lap. *"Sí."*

"And you want me to feed this delusion, I presume?" He has lost the collegial tone he has begun to use with her in the shop. Now he speaks in the familiar voice of all the suppers Vini can remember—stern, mocking. "Perhaps we should take the marionette to church tomorrow? Invite our friends to a baptism?"

"Mama needs time, that is all."

"Time?"

"I was blind for weeks, Papa." She wants to touch his arm, but knows he will only pull away. "Mama will open her eyes soon. She will see the baby is a puppet. But for now she needs to see with her heart."

"And what does she see, pray tell?" Prospero reaches for the cup he has put down, takes another sip. "What does she see when she looks at that pathetic wooden doll?"

How can he understand? *Look first with your eyes, garzoni.* "She does not see a puppet, Father. She sees the gift she has prayed to give you." *Use them like hands, figli. Caress every curve, every corner.* "She sees her love for you made flesh. She sees all your fondest hopes realized at last."

"This is nonsense that must not be indulged, Daughter." He is the padre of her childhood, the unreachable arbiter. "This is a weak woman's fancy."

"No, Papa. It is a strong woman's dream." Some use paint; some use clay; Mama has used her body and her boundless love.

"I will not involve myself in this travesty." When he discusses perspective and hue, Father is calm, self-assured. But now his face is angry, trapped. Vini sees the hint of fear she saw on the stairs the evening he almost visited Mama. "I will not take part in your puppet show."

"You will." She has not planned to say this. She has planned to honor his pride, his pain.

"What?" Prospero's anger is cut short by surprise. In all her fifteen years, Vini has never challenged him before. She has painted behind his back. She has talked Paolo into representing her work as his own. But she has never defied Father to his face. She has never given him an order.

"You will help Mama, Papa." She does not study her hands now but looks at him, eye to eye. "Because if you do not do this for her, I will never paint again." Eye to eye. "And if I cannot paint, there will be no Fontana in your studio."

He says nothing, only stares. *Can he know how much this costs her? Can he know that if she does not paint, she will turn gnarled and stunted like a plant without sun? She may marry. She may have babes of her own. She may sew and dance and wear fine clothes to church. But she will never again go where she needs to go, be who she must be.*

It is not a time you could count, even if you were standing under the tower clock. It happens faster than a breath, than a hope. Father sees it in her face. He measures her love: he knows Vini is prepared to give up the career she has begun. And he knows it will be the hardest thing she has ever done.

Then Mama appears at the door. Her hair is swept back and braided twice around her head. She is dressed in green silk with lace panels at the bodice and skirt. Her earrings and the strand of pearls at her throat glow with a dim luster, dwarfed by the light in her eyes.

It is not a light that shines out, so much as it draws everything else in. Vini and her father cannot turn away from Antonia once she steps into the room. They cannot take their eyes from her lovliness, her breathtaking motherhood.

She carries the puppet, dressed in a white gown, to Prospero. She stands before him and waits, as if she is making an offering in church. Father rises slowly from his seat. Like a sleepwalker, he holds out his arms and Mama sets the puppet in them.

Papa cradles the wooden prince as awkwardly as he would a real child, his eyes fixed on his wife's face. In his own countenance, Vini sees wonder and, even more, a sort of timid reverence. He, too, is in church. Finally Antonia's joy, her relentless light, vanquishes him; he swallows, turns away from her, stares instead at the puppet.

"He will be baptized Prospero, of course," Mama says. "But I hope you will let us call him 'Pero."

Father continues to look into the painted smile. "I think . . ."

"He has your eyes, no?"

"He is—"

"And if he has your hands," Antonia says, "he can be a famous painter."

When Papa looks at Vini, before he turns back to the doll, she sees the shine in his eyes. If someone had asked her before today, she would have told them that Prospero Fontana never cries.

"He is a handsome child." Father says the words slowly, haltingly, as if he were just learning to speak. "Whatever his future, he is fortunate indeed to have such a mother." Again he turns to look at Vini. If he were not holding the puppet, she knows he would brush away the tears that threaten to spill down his face. "And such a sister."

If he had crushed Mama, had waved away her dream, Vini would have done as she promised; she would have laid down her brush. But, oh, sweet Lord who knows our hearts, the relief that floods her now makes the room lose its substance, makes the moment thin and swell like the skin of a bubble, opening, opening. She will paint again.

Father hands the tiny figure in its long gown back to Antonia, and then he does just what Vini has imagined. Roughly, as if he is wiping away the sweat of a workday, he dabs at his eyes. "I think it unlikely," he tells his wife, "that our son could match our daughter's talent." He turns to Vini again, wearing the same look he wore the day her sight returned, the same stunned gratitude. "Or her heart."

"You are right, of course." Mother hugs her babe close. "Perhaps our son will be a scholar, then." She stares fondly at the wooden face. "Or he may practice the art of healing." Her lip trembles as she looks up from the toy. "The world is so full of suffering, my dear."

There is that stern expression again, that shadow of fear, before Prospero speaks. But then, gingerly, he slips his arm around his wife's waist. "Come, let us sit down, 'Tonia." He helps her to the table as Silvana and Betta hurry in from the kitchen to set the cradle on the floor.

Dizzy with revelation, Vini studies the faces before her. At the head of the table sits her father, her teacher, her colleague, her benefactor. *You have said it, Papa. Now you have proved it. You believe in me, and that feels like grace.*

Across from Vini sits her mother, blessed with a wisdom Prospero's apprentices will never learn. *You have taught me so much, Mama. Even when I did not listen.*

Papa finishes the rolled mutton and cabbage, eating self-consciously, careful not to find fault. Antonia watches him the whole time, gently rocking the cradle between them. And in this movement, the steady, slow back-and-forth, Vini sees the simple shape of love.

As if she understands, Antonia turns to Vini. "I hope we will tend the flowers this summer," she says, her cheeks flushed like a child's. For a moment her eyes find the hands in her lap, but now she is smiling again at her daughter. It is not the haunted smile she has worn for days, but the sweet, open look Vini remembers from their secret garden. "Just the two of us, eh?"

"Oh, yes, Mama!" Vini's fork stays where it is. She is too full to take a single bite. "We will not forget your flowers!" Her mother will get well, she knows that now. She wishes she could tell Papa. She wants to put a finger on the place where his brows meet, wants to smooth away that fierce line.

But perhaps he already knows. Because now Prospero Fontana lifts his glass to make a toast. "Let us drink to art," he says. He nods at Vini, then at Antonia. "And to life."

She dreamed she was the princess puppet again, but instead of a gown she wore Bradamante's shining armor. It made a satisfactory clinking sound whenever she walked.

She had just taken off her gloves and was admiring her own white hands, brilliant as lilies, when the prince, beside her, clutched one to his chest, holding it fast with a kiss. Next to him, the duke and duchess, who had tired of chasing each other around the stage, stood still, their arms entwined. The duke began to declaim, loudly and persuasively, about something, though when she woke, she could not remember a single word he had said. Behind them, an old serving woman with no teeth laughed uproariously whenever he paused for breath.

It occurred to Princess Bradamante that her dragon was missing, and though the others were too busy listening to the duke's speech to notice, she was delighted when a small creature with a spiked tail and wings came scuttling toward her from behind the curtains. He was now the size of a lapdog, but she recognized the dragon as soon as he roared to be picked up and then scrubbed her nose with his rough tongue.

She was surprised to observe, after she set him down, that the tiny dragon was balanced on his hind legs, with no one controlling his dance. But what amazed her more, what made her sob with joy, was to find that she could raise her own white hand, could wiggle her lily fingers, without any strings at all.

After Words: The Facts Behind This Fiction

I was raised in a family of painters. When I was little, my picture books were my parents' volumes of Renaissance art. In college I had a double major, in English literature and art history. I paint myself, and even had a sculpture studio for several years. None of this training, though, prepared me for "meeting" Vini six years ago at the National Museum of Women in the Arts, in Washington, D.C.

Neither the books I'd read nor the courses I'd studied had done much to dissuade me from the notion that all great Renaissance painters were male. Imagine my surprise, then, when I discovered that the artist featured in the museum's one-woman show could hold her own against many of the Renaissance "giants" I'd studied. Although she died more than four hundred years ago, Lavinia Fontana painted with a delight in surfaces and a wry sense of humor that seemed surprisingly "modern." Her canvases made my mouth water!

Although I never intended to write a book about her (my other fiction has contemporary settings), I found myself learning everything I could about Vini over the next four years. I learned that by the time she died, in 1614, she had become a virtual legend in her native Italy and throughout Europe. I learned that she trained in her father's studio and eventually married one of his students, a certain Gian Paolo Zappi.

A mediocre painter who recognized his wife's genius, Zappi gave up his career to promote her work and help raise their eleven (yes, eleven!) children. Vini undertook more than 130 major paintings, including altarpieces, private portraits, and papal commissions. The family eventually moved to Rome, where nobility, clergy, and foreign courts all became her patrons.

Vini supported her father, who died in 1592, and her mother, who lived into her eighties. While she enjoyed more fame than any female artist before her (and most since), she suffered several personal tragedies: only three of her children outlived her, and one of her daughters was blinded in an accident.

Vini obtained a university degree, was admitted to the Roman Academy, and had a medal struck in her honor. More than thirty of her paintings survive today, work that reveals a deep sensitivity to her sitters' emotions; an unabashed love of textures, jewelry, and dress; and a subtle humor that animates her portraits of women, children, and small dogs.

I found a chance to visit Vini's hometown two years ago. I prowled Balogna's galleries and explored the streets Vini and her family must have walked. I became convinced I was meant to tell her story when, on the last day of my stay, I met an elderly priest who let me into the back of a closed church where one of Vini's altar paintings still hangs.

My Italian is, at best, pathetic; the priest's English was nonexistent. But the two of us stood in front of the painting (*Birth of the Virgin Mary*—look it up and check out the light!) and shared our reactions, slowly, haltingly. He showed me Vini's signature in the lower right-hand corner; we joked about the little dog that ran across the bottom of the canvas; I told him about Vini's life; he told me how the congregation had once lost this painting when it was loaned out for an exhibit, and how they were determined never to let it go again.

As I left the church and headed to the train station, I heard Vini whispering in my ear, for perhaps the hundredth time since we'd met. "Now, Luisa?" she asked. "Now can we start the book?"

Historical fiction is hard. There is legwork, research, endless fact-checking. And there is waiting time, too, the simmering while everything you've learned becomes second nature, so that you are finally, really *there.* I understood that all this lay ahead of me, but I understood, too, that what we don't know about Vini is more intriguing than what the record shows: How did a young girl, raised in the strictly ordered atmosphere of the Counter-Reformation, grow into a savvy, political, gifted public figure? What made her father take her on as an apprentice in his all-male studio? Where did this woman find the courage, grace, and agility to compete and succeed where few females had ever been allowed?

Because there is no historical record of Lavinia's adolescence, I was free to "make up" Vini, the teenager; to speculate about the early experiences and emotions that might have shaped Lavinia, the woman: Without modern birth control, most Renaissance families were large. Was Vini an only child because her mother suffered miscarriages? Maybe. Measles can and did cause temprorary blindness. Was Vini's love of surfaces and textures fed by a period of being unable to see? Maybe. Did Vini resort to subterfuge to join her father's *bottega*? Maybe.

Puppets, scorpions, tarot cards, beggars at Mass—they all existed in Vini's time. Did Vini experience them? Maybe. Maybes of course, are the stuff of fiction, the reason Vini's story fascinated me. "Okay, okay," I told my new protagonist as I boarded the train out of Bologna. She was still whispering in my ear, and I knew she wouldn't stop until we explained how Vini had become Lavinia. "We start the book tomorrow."

And we did.

Louise Bower